# CUL-DE-SAC

PAUL HOWARTH

# DEDICATIONS

To my wife Helen who has always backed me in anything I have chosen to do.

To my parents Margaret and John who I can always rely on when in need of support, or in my father's case comic relief.

To my dog Max who was always the very goodest of boys, sleep well my friend.

To anyone who was ever laughed at when they said they were going to do something crazy like write a book.

This is dedicated to you all for being part of a world where this is possible.

# CONTENTS

# CHAPTER 1:
# THE SCRATCHES

Little did Hank Johnson know while patrolling the porch of his house on Vernon's Place in the autumn of 1983 with the rain lashing down on the now pond like road with bloated gutters and leaf clogged drains, that today would be the beginning of the horrors that would be spoken about for generations to come.

"I will make sure Ravi hears about this you little piss ant" he shouted towards young Tommy Killinger the local paperboy as he rode out of sight into the misty rain made fog that morning, you see every morning Tommy would come along on his old silver rusty BMX with its shiny new wheel and one of those long flags all the kids seemed to have on them, he'd sit bang smack in the middle of the circular cul-de-sac and toss papers to four of the five houses there. No one lived at number 3 and hadn't for a very long time not since the 'incident' as the residents called it, however today that would change with the arrival of some new neighbours from England. Anyway you may be wondering what is wrong with Tommy doing that? Well – nothing except Hanks paper always seemed to land perfectly in a pothole on his driveway which brimmed with rainwater and mud, sure they were wrapped in plastic bags to protect them but Hank's always seemed to be torn open.

"I am telling you Martha the little shit does it on purpose, he has never forgiven me for reversing over his bloody bike even after I replaced the damn wheel" Hank said as he struggled huffing away like an old steam train bending down to pick up the sodden paper. As he stood up his large stomach hung over the top of his pyjama bottoms protruding below the tightly fastened shirt with bulging buttons like a dog's tongue just poking from its mouth.

"For god sake man the boy is only eight he's hardly plotting to take you down one paper at a time is he! Now get in here, look at those bottoms soaked through again" the dumpy rosy cheeked Martha said. The rains had been hitting hard the past few days and Vernon's Place felt it more than most as it sat at the bottom of a slight slope which led into the tree covered cul-de-sac, Hank who lived at number 4 and Stu from number 1 had earlier in the week put a few sand bags in front of the abandoned number 3 as that was in line with the road leading in from Pontins Street and it took the brunt of the flowing streams cascading down.

The house had sat empty for at least 15 maybe even 20 years, no one wanted to buy it after its last occupants were murdered by their own daughter who then took her own life. The Residents Association which comprised of the people living in the other 4 houses had staunchly maintained the grounds of the house and even its exterior all these years to maintain the high standards of their immaculately kept street,

Hank even bought a new petrol chainsaw to chop back some trees that had began to intrude on the houses personal space.

"Do you think I should warn them?"

"Warn them? Warn who, about what?"

"The English about the boy" Hank said.

"I think I should warn them about you! Now for god sake go and get changed out of those wet clothes or it won't be the boy who finishes you off it will be pneumonia" Martha said with a hint of early morning frustration rattling from her voice, some would say she deserved a medal for dealing with Hank, they had been married for 20 years or more and she has gone through it all with him from the time he thought the mafia was stealing his milk off their doorstep because he called an Italian fella who cut him up at a junction a greaseball, to the time he forgot he had taken a book from the library and was convinced someone was trying to frame him for book theft.

Hank was harmless enough if not a little erratic, and suspicious of everyone new to his life – as leader of the Residents Association it came as part of the territory, or that's what he would tell people anyway. As he buttoned his shirt he heard the grumbling of an engine and the distinctive sound of the gutter water spraying the pavement, looking from the front bedroom window and by looking I mean peeping through a very tiny gap at the side of the net privacy curtains he saw a large blue van with 'International Movers Ltd' in large white letters on the side pull up to number 3. He watched on as two scrawny looking men with hair that could only be described as looking like busted mattresses hopped out of the cab one straight into a huge pool of water which in turn soaked his tatty well used boots.

"Surely these two couldn't be the newbie's" Hank uttered to himself rather condescendingly, this was a very respectable little burb of the town and they would most surely bring the bar down in his eyes. Thankfully the voice of reason soon put him at rest

"Don't panic dear they are just dropping the furniture off" Martha said. Hank nodded with an air of relief remembering that when he quizzed the realtor, the workmen and the window fitters  they all confirmed it was a married couple moving in so there was no need to fear any wild parties or god forbid orgies, because in Hanks eyes that's what would happen with two fellas of that age living together.

As Hank watched on hiding behind his net curtains, Gene from number 5 came out to greet the removal men, Gene was an older guy in his 60's. He lived with his friend Alf they had lived on Vernon's since they were kids, Alf lived at number 1 for most of his life until his wife Gladys passed away which happened to be around the same time Gene lost Mary and the two friends decided to move in together rather that rattle around in two rather empty homes, so Alf sold up to Stu and Jenny.

"Morning chaps, let me open up for you"

"Thanks pops, we want to get this stuff off that van and in ASAP, I don't enjoy working in this damn rain"

"I don't blame you boys – now you know where it's all going right?" Gene said as he thrust the now unlocked garage door open, they nodded and he scurried to the front door to open that up, he had a small smirk on his face as despite Hanks best attempts he could see the twitching of the curtains and knew it would be driving him mad as to why Gene had keys to number 3. In reality it was a simple answer he knew the realtor Debbie Shultz, she was huge in this area and was now a goddess at her office for managing to sell the 'murder house'. She had asked Gene if he would help with the furniture delivery as the new owners wouldn't be arriving until later that day and she had been called away on a family emergency typically as the other staff were unavailable for the weekend.

As the door opened Gene peeked in to see how the renovations had gone, everything was immaculate like the wrapping had just been taken off, it was a far throw from the damp stinking pit it had been inside for the past 15 plus years

"You can put lipstick on a pig but it's still a pig" is what Jenny from number 1 would remark as the residents tirelessly maintained the plot over the years. The residents, Gene included had watched for the best part of 8 months as tradesmen and fitters came and went so they knew about the dark wood flooring, the new kitchen and the cream coloured paint that went in there but not how it would look

"Bland" Gene scoffed as he saw the cream coloured walls I mean no wall paper? My god these Brits are odd folks!

The two men soon shuffled past Gene with a large brown sofa with four square wooden legs ready to clang into any shins brave enough to get close to them.

"Shit! – is that us?" Andy who seemed to be the brains of the operation asked Ben the younger slightly vacant looking fellow with some remains of that morning's breakfast staining his off white t-shirt, he was referring to 3 scratch marks on the new perfectly polished and buffed wooden floor.

"Uh – uh – must of been! Damn it Andy I'm sorry I didn't even feel it touch the floor or nothing"

"Don't worry lads, I have some wood polish at home when you're done I will get it sorted and if they notice I will tell them it was like that when we opened up the door" Gene said, he shot them a reassuring wink and the two men brimming with relief carried on with more care into the lounge to sit the sofa down. As they went to fetch more items from the van Andy looked down at the scratches thinking to himself they didn't really look like furniture scratches more like –

"Andy come on man this table weighs a damn ton" Ben yelled from the van, to which Andy shook his head and with it an uncomfortable feeling and headed to Ben's aid.

As the hours ticked by the rain began to drift away in the afternoon winds, the trickling of water rolling almost rhythmically down the sloped entrance to Vernon's Place and was accompanied by the gentle rustling of the remaining autumn leaves. A loud rattling noise signalled that the removals van was being shut up - Andy and Ben would soon be on their way, they had been instructed to leave items in certain rooms where possible but they didn't need to place them out because the English would do that, then as instructed by Debbie Shultz in a note left on the kitchen worktop returned the keys to Gene.

"Don't worry boys, I will sort that floor out before they arrive" he said before tapping the side of the van as they pulled away. Gene headed to his garage at pace, an almost frustrated air about his demeanour. He rattled around in his garage which was more like a store, shelves in rows carefully laid out in an almost maze like formation that clearly over the years had become less organised. Cans of half used bug sprays and adhesive clattered to the floor like the final crescendo of a grand orchestra

"For the love of god I swear you can never find anything in this bloody house" he said just before crashing his slightly balding head against the upper shelf

"Bastard!"

"Excuse me?" a voice from behind asked with a hint of slight amusement to it

"I assume you have lost something – again" Alf who you could almost mistaken for Gene in the dim lighting of the garage due to their similar appearance and it had happen a few times, had come to investigate the clattering as they'd had issues with a local cat getting into his fishing supplies recently.

"The floor wax, I can't find the bloody floor wax"

"What on earth do you need that for?"

"Number 3 there are some scratches on the floor still, the removal men are worried they will be blamed for it" Gene said.

"Ah – well have you tried under the sink?" – Gene went over to a small unit in the garage with an old tin sink in it, the taps tapped up after what you'd assume was years of use through tinkering with manly things. He opened the stiff squeaky door reached in and pulled out the can and shook it in Alf's general direction as he smiled. He grabbed some brushes and cloths and headed back over to number 3, all under the watchful eye of Hank who had now moved to the armchair situated by his large front window.

Over the years Gene had amassed a variety of skills so buffing out some scratches on the wooden floor wasn't too much of an issue, they were deeper than they looked when stood above them but he managed to ensure they were barely visible unless someone pointed them out and then just hoped that the English put a runner down or something to cover them. As he packed away his kit and cleared the mess he had caused he glanced towards the freshly painted white stair banisters which sat to the left just opposite the entrance and noticed specs of what appeared to be red paint across the sides of the bottom step, but from detailed description Hank had provided of all that entered the house there had been no mention of red paint at all. A chill shot down his spine as he mumbled nervously to himself while snatching at a cloth from his pocket and dampening it with spit to start rubbing away the marks. With the sound of a car approaching Gene hastily crammed everything into a small carrier bag and hurried out the door fumbling to lock it, just as he left a yellow taxi sat with its doors open, he rushed away with his head down as if he hadn't noticed it hoping that he would go un-noticed also.

# CHAPTER 2:
# A NOTE FROM DEBBIE SHULTZ

The loud pop of the champagne cork which could be likened to the last cry of a thousand balloons echoed around the small offices of Bishops Homes & Rentals, after 15 years, 10 months and 11 days Number 3 Vernon's Place or the 'murder house' as it was known in the office had finally been sold. Debbie Shultz a slim 48 year old with dazzling white teeth and golden hair who had been poached from rivals Jenkins & Son just 6 months previous had finally managed to sell the poisoned challis, she had pushed hard to advertise some of the abandoned properties overseas as 'fixer uppers' to people looking to move to America. It was a long process as it took weeks for the adverts to be published in newspapers then longer for interested parties to request a pack with the homes in and receive them, but this had made it all worth it.

Max and Amy Jones from England had spotted a grainy black and white picture of number 3 in their paper and instantly fell in love, it looked immaculately kept from the outside and was framed almost artistically by the many trees that dressed the whole street. Debbie took the risk of being totally open in the pack but English don't scare easily their reply was along the lines of – *As long as the bodies aren't still in there we will take it!* The Jones's laid out what they wanted and how they wanted it to Debbie who managed the whole renovation for a modest fee of course.

The months drifted by like a feather surfing a gentle breeze and every tradesman and delivery service you could think of passed through the house under the un-resting supervision of Miss Shultz, you see this was her first crack at project management for a client and she had gotten a taste for it and the fee she would collect too. She often passed a small boutique in town with a gleaming pair of red high heeled shoes in the window that once the Jones's had moved in and were happy she would reward herself with, she had no partner not because of looks because believe me she was a stunner - long smooth legs always framed with an immaculately kept pinstriped skirt, you noticed those legs before anything else! No it was not her looks that kept her single it was more the fear of a female who was successful, many men feared such a woman through their own narrow minded views. Her family all lived by the coast a few hours' drive away, so the only person she really could treat or receive a treat from was herself.

As June came along Max arrived to finally meet Debbie and see the progress of the renovations, none of the residents really paid much attention as they were so used to people coming and going it was part of the daily routine now. *Another tradesman*, Hank the Residents Associations chief curtain twitcher thought as he saw Max a tall, lean well kept man chatting humorously with Miss Shultz. Amy was unable to join him so Max came armed to the teeth with about 10 reels of camera film, and photoed almost every inch of the house, and the outside for that matter. He couldn't wait for Amy to see the progress along with family, friends and neighbours back home who fell into one of two categories; a) brimming with excitement for the pair or b) completely jealous and hoping a storm sends a tree crashing through the roof.

"You have gone above and beyond Debbie, you really have. If it carries on like this we will be in sooner than we thought"

"I am so happy you feel that way, I have to admit I was a little worried having your whole future in my hands to a degree, it was a tad daunting" she said.

"Well if you hadn't of told me I'd of thought you'd overseen hundreds of renovations, you really have done amazingly well". Debbie gleamed as Max's soothing British tone almost caressed her ears, they say that certain voices can have an almost hypnotic effect on people and right then that was the case, not in a sexual way but just in a hell yeh, job satisfaction kind of way. Max stayed in town for a few days to see some of the work and explore the local area, whispers in town of a nice Englishman were met with grumblings from Hank who couldn't believe he had missed out on striking up a conversation with the soon to be newbie on the block and when I say conversation I mean more of a third degree.

A few more months passed by and it was getting closer to moving in day, the trees had become a little wild and Gene had offered to cut them back as usual, however Hank had purchased a brand new top of the range petrol chainsaw to make short work of them because as he often reminded Gene

"You have to look after yourself, you're not as young as you used to be and ladders are risky for men of advancing years". It was always an awkward moment but one Gene seemed to take in his stride as he often did, with the trees cut back and the lawns mowed by Stu for the last time all was set for the English's arrival this coming weekend.

Debbie always liked to do a last sense check before her clients moved in so at around 10pm Friday evening she headed over to number 3 and stood silently in the freshly painted lobby area, running her had down the smooth pearl white banister the smell of paint faintly entertaining her senses

"Well done Debbie" she said to herself as she walked through the open squared arch into the lounge, as with the other homes in the cul-de-sac the lounge was accessible from two openings one to the left of the entrance adjacent to the stairs and another into the kitchen which could be seen from the lobby with the dining room off to the right.

As Debbie stood in the lounge tirelessly checking every inch of paintwork she heard what sounded like the closing of the front door

"Hello" she said as she returned to the lobby

"Is anyone there?" – silence – *I must of left it ajar* –she thought to herself as she headed to the kitchen, at that moment from the corner of her eye she could of swore she saw something move across the lobby behind her in the reflection of the kitchen window. She spun around.

"H-Hello" she asked with a tremble shacking her words – again silence.

"If this is some kids messing around you aren't

funny" still a deafly silence fell only the increasingly pacey sound of her own breath accentuated by the empty and echo filled kitchen could be heard. *Pull yourself together* she thought, after all she had done these late night checks a thousand times and only ever had one issue with Bobby some jumped up little shit from the 'wrong side of the tracks' when she worked in Brooklyn for a time. He tried to scare her for a bet with friends and it worked to a degree until her then boyfriend who was waiting for her outside in the car heard her scream and knocked ten shades of shit out of the 14 year old, there was a whole court case and everything but Bobby's reputation worked heavily against him and to be honest I think the cops thought he deserved it.

As she shook her head in disbelief at herself she looked down and noticed what looked like a chip on one of the cabinet doors in front of the window, she bent down to take a look running her finger along the edge and a small bit of saw dust dropped to the floor a sense of relief washed over her, sure it wasn't anything major but she wanted no little niggles or issues for the Jones's, she raised herself to her feet and the relief soon turned to sheer terror as in the window reflection she could see over her shoulder a man dressed in all black with just a pair of cold eyes gleaming in the dim light, for what felt like an eternity she stared frozen with fear at the reflection her stomach churned erratically, her body almost tingled in a way that made her feel like she wanted to tear her skin off, then fight or flight seemed to kick in and in the briefest moment of clarity she stamped one of her high heels right onto the man in blacks foot. He growled through his teeth as he fell back slightly and

Debbie shuffled as fast as possible in her heels through the lounge she looked over her shoulder briefly and saw the man at the kitchen archway she headed for the lobby and the door but as she got towards the archway at the bottom of the stairs she hit a wall of black spun round and crashed to the floor banging her head as she landed. How the hell had he gotten there so quick? It was almost superhuman to get from the kitchen archway to the entrance area so fast.

"Now you could scream, but I wouldn't suggest it" the man said in an almost growl like gruff voice, as he did so he slowly raised a knife from the back of his jet black combat looking bottoms

"Because if you did I would take this and ram it in your cunt and slice you open from bottom to the top"

Debbie began to uncontrollably sob as she looked up in horror, her visual of the man had become disjointed and blurred as tears swelled up and then cascaded down her cheek dragging mascara with them

"Wh-what do y-you want f-from me?" she said.

"You, Oh dear sweet Debbie you have played your part in this little game perfectly, you have done everything I needed you to and you don't even realise it – So much so that I may even reward you when this is all over"

The house which moments before had felt like a bright, fresh and joyful place now felt like a prison to Debbie who lay blood dripping from a small cut on the side of her forehead like the drips of a bathroom sink late at night *Tap – Tap – Tap* the blood could be heard in the silence as she processed what she had just heard

"H-How have I helped, I-I don't understand" she said.

"Well of course not my dear because you didn't know you were helping did you, for a good while now patience has been needed for this house to sell I even started to think it wasn't going to happen then Debbie Shultz turns up with her tight tops and pencil skirts and bingo we have a sale" the man walked over to the stairs and sat on the bottom step

"You see that was key this house needed to be sold, there needed to be an unknown entity in this game and all the other ass holes in this little sac know each other inside and out – there needed to be uncertainty"

Debbie now resembling something from a Kiss fan club as blood and mascara covered her face, visibly tried to process what was being said

"But why" she said

"Why do you want new people here I don't understand"

"Well if I told you that I would have to kill you" the man laughed sinisterly as he rose to his feet again with the knife gripped in his hand, Debbie winced and shuffled back slightly her eyes clenched tightly shut.

"But no Debbie I need more from you so let's get started shall we" the man said, he grabbed her by the ankles and began to drag her towards the basement door situated under the stairs Debbie made the hint of what would be a scream

"What the fuck did I tell you bitch? Scream and I will open you up like a fucking fish" he then pulled a manky old cloth from his pocket and rammed it in her mouth which made her choke and gag for a second. Then he again began to drag her by her ankles she dug her nails into the wooden floor so tightly she got a splinter under her nail the pain making her pull her hand away, as she slid helplessly past the stairs she coughed the motion of which sprayed small droplets of blood on the bottom step. At the basement doorway the man dragged her to her feet and pointed the knife to the back of her neck

"Down there" he said ushering her into the basement lit only by a solitary light bulb shadows engulfing the bare brick walls, a small table with a chair sat perfectly in the middle of the room, he removed the rag from her mouth

"Sit", Debbie adjusted her skirt and sat in the small metal camping chair.

"Now Debbie, if you do what's needed here you will be fine – ok"

"Y-Yes – yes whatever you want just please don't hurt me" she said.

"Good, I need you to write me three notes, one to your boss saying there has been a family emergency and you've had to leave town"

"But why you said I'd be ok if I ..."

"Just fucking write it and you will be" the man said

"A second simply saying I have had to leave town for family reasons can you sort the removal men out and pass the keys to the new owners. And a third for the removal men telling them to return the keys to whoever let them in, feel free to bulk it out a bit, then sign it from you"

Debbie started to write but began shaking frantically

"That's no good Debbie, now don't get this mixed up, the notes in your handwriting makes it more authentic but I swear to god I will slice your face off and do them myself if I have to! Now try again" She took a deep breath and steadied herself then began to write what had been demanded. The man watched over her shoulder as she scrawled beautifully on the note paper.

"I've done what you asked now p-please let me go" she slumped in her chair sobbing as she said it knowing that her request was more likely than not futile.

"Sorry Deb, it doesn't quite work that way you see I need you out the way while the games in play honey. I'm going to take you in your car to a little place I have out in the woods very secure so you can't do anything silly, I will check on you every day bring you plenty of food and water, stuff to read" He then stopped, and looked Debbie in the eyes, everything seemed to slow down for her, her heart beat thudding in her chest like it wanted to break out and run.

"You know what" the man said

"That's a lot of fucking work" then in an instant he slashed the knife across Debbie's throat, her swelling tear filled eyes widened almost cartoon like in size she fell to the floor clawing at her throat trying to stop the blood that oozed through her fingers, choking, spluttering and convulsing on the floor the man knelt by her.

"Maybe if you hadn't rejected me you stuck up bitch I'd of let you live" the man pulled down the black mask covering his lower face and as life left her body Debbie realised the man was someone she had known and trusted.

As morning arrived three notes had been left from Debbie one on the desk of Frederick Bishop the owner of Bishops Homes & Rentals, one for the removal men and one that sat poking out of the mailbox of Gene Raymond and Alf Greenway with a set of keys that had a tag attached *No.3 Vernon's Place/Jones* scribbled on it in black pen. As Gene studied the note in his slippers and dressing gown Dennis Thompson who lived at number 2 with his wife Cara was out for his morning run, he jogged over his red curled hair poking above a bright freshly washed white sweatband his white socks pulled up almost stretching to below his knees – the less said about the small blue shorts the better.

"Anything interesting Gene" he said while doing some stretches.

"Hey Dennis –erm – it's Debbie the realtor for number 3, she has been called away on a family emergency and her colleagues are all off so she has asked me to see to the removal men and hand the keys over to the new folks"

"I bet that will go down well with Hank when he finds out" Dennis laughed

"He will be quizzing her on why he wasn't asked"

"Oh I will look forward to that one" Gene said

"I just hope all is ok with Debbie"
"I'm sure it will be, right I best get on see you later Gene" Dennis jogged off as Gene threw him a half hearted wave still fixated to the note.

Later that day after the hustle and bustle of the furniture and possessions being delivered, Gene shot through the door of his house almost causing Alf to have heart failure

"What the hell is wrong with you ? you look like you've seen a ghost" Alf said.

"N-Nothing just a few splashes that needed cleaning up at number 3, some sloppy clean up yesterday I think, I shit myself though as I left I think their taxi just pulled in and I didn't want them to see me with this cleaning stuff leaving their house"

"Well I'm sure if they ask they will understand when you explain about the keys and all that" Alf said, the two men moved to the window and indeed saw a the tall immaculately kept figure of Max Jones his arm around the shorter but just as well kept Amy as they gazed upon their American dream

"Right I suppose I best head over and introduce myself and explain what's happened" Gene said, he swept up the keys took a deep breath and headed over to greet the new neighbours.

# CHAPTER 3:
# MEET THE JONES'S

A cold prickly breeze brushed by the faces of Max and Amy Jones as they stood in childlike awe of their beautiful new home the freshly painted porch and newly fitted door and windows that sparkled in the sun which was now breaking through following the rains earlier in the day, the smell of wet freshly cut grass engulfed them as they breathed every moment in. The couple had been through some tough times lately just a year pervious to the move Amy had lost their first child and a few months after that Max who was a professional football player or soccer as his knew neighbours would know it, had retired at just 28 years old due to injury, the insurance payout is what had funded the dream move.

They never let on but the pair knew there was plenty of curtain twitching from the surrounding houses going on. *My god she could be a damn bikini model with that figure* Jenny Patterson, Stu Patterson from number 1's wife thought as she gave the new youngest wife on the block the once over, you see the Jones's were now the babies of the sac, the others were in their late 30's early 40's apart from Gene and Alf who were both 60 plus.

"Baby the moment we step over that threshold

our new life can really begin, a fresh start with new dreams and better memories to be made" Amy said as she looked adoringly into Max's eyes.

"I can't wait" he said

"But – we can't go anywhere until Debbie arrives and it's not like her to be late" at that point from behind them they heard a faint

"Excuse me – er – hi – hello, My name is Gene – Gene Raymond I live at number 5" Gene extended his hand to Max and then Amy who reciprocated slightly confused but in typical English polite manner.

"I am sorry but Debbie has been suddenly called away, a family emergency I believe" Gene said

"The other members of her office are off until Monday so she dropped your keys to me with a note, I hope you don't mind but I took care of the furniture arrival and locked up for you"

"Oh wow – thank you Mr. Raymond that's really kind of you" Max said

"Sorry where are my manners, I am Max, Max Jones and this is my wife Amy"

"Please call me Gene I insist, and nice to meet you both, I am just hoping I got them to put everything roughly in the right places for you"

"I'm sure it's all fine, I just hope Debbie is ok. I will call her office Monday if I don't hear from her" Max said

"Luckily nothing needed signing I guess"

"I'm sure she will be in touch, she is a good one that woman" Gene said gesturing towards the house as if to back up what a great job she had done.

"My lord look at me keeping you out here with when all you will want to do is get inside your new home! Here are the keys and welcome to Vernon's Place, if you need anything I'm at number 5 with my friend Alf" Gene placed the keys into Max's hands and smiled to them both as he turned back to head home.

The couple climbed the 6 stone steps up to the porch and Max passed the keys to Amy

"You open up honey" he said as a loving smile bloomed on his face.

"Hey – Hi – er – er Hello" Hank came bundling from his front door still pulling on his left boot as the he stumbled down the steps and headed over

"I am Hank Johnson, founding member and head of The Residents Association here to welcome you to Vernon's Place" he grabbed Max's arm and shook it almost as if they had been glued together and he was trying to shake free, he then let go and Max's hand flew up from the momentum. Hank grabbed Amy by the shoulders and slammed a huge kiss on her right cheek she could of claimed for whiplash it hit her so hard.

"Oh my, well thank you Mr Johnson and hello to you too! I am Amy Jones and this is my husband Max" Hank gleefully nodded at them both, Max was rubbing his shoulder wondering if it was still in its socket.

"Please call me Hank kids, if you need anything I am always here 24/7 – 365 days a year but I do like to sleep in on a Sunday" he snorted as he laughed, The Jones's politely laughed but it was more at him in a nervous way than with him but Hank was too excited to notice, he then stood just smiling at them as they did to him, it was awkward for the couple but also they were trying not to burst into hysterics.

"Hey Hank, this has been great but I would love to finally show Amy our new home if it's all the same to you" Max said.

"Of course son, I will get out of your hair remember I'm at number 4 with my Martha" he shot them a thumbs up and walked back towards home Martha watching him from the lounge window with a look of embarrassment and apology on her face.

"Shall we?" Amy said putting her hand on the key which sat patiently in the lock waiting to be turned.

"Well howdy there you must be the Brits" Dennis said huffing from his run, the key was released again and the polite smiles resurfaced as the couple turned to return the hellos

"Don't worry I won't chew your ears off like I'm sure Hank has! I just wanted to say hi as I spotted y'all, as ever if you need anything just drop by number 2 My wife Cara or myself are happy to help" he said

"y'all have a good day" he jogged off and again Amy placed her hand on the key.

The couple hesitated for a moment and even turned around to see if anyone was approaching – nothing not a soul was around, Amy turned the key and nudged the door open her eyes widened like a child taken to a toyshop for the first time, it was so bright and the dark wood floors made it feel warm and cosy. Max swooped Amy off her feet and stepped inside he then kissed her softly on the lips

"Welcome home" he said as they smiled and kissed again before Max threw her playfully onto the new sofa still in its protective wrappings, he sat next to her and placed his hand on her knee and gave it a squeeze

"Where the hell do you think the kettle is" he said before both fell into a sleep deprived fit of laugher.

As the days rolled by they consisted of furniture being placed and replaced in a plethora of different areas around the house, particularly a round black side table which went on a grand tour of the lounge about 3 times before settling in the first place it ever rested in the Jones's new home, the lounge corner next to a brown leather armchair covered in a cream blanket. The chair sat next to the large front window which had a shelved unit under it housing a record player, some records and a variety of books stacked neatly along the bottom shelf. There had also been copious visits from neighbours with care packages of food and toiletries to make the strenuous move more bearable, they particularly enjoyed Martha Johnson's lasagne but that came at a cost as when Martha visited so did Hank – and by this point they were sure he had explored more of the house than they had.

Max had been trying to reach Debbie Shultz since Monday, he had been heading down to the phone box on Pontins each day but her office hadn't heard from her and didn't have a contact number for her family. Max hadn't paid her for the renovation management yet and it wasn't run through Bishops Homes & Rentals so he didn't want to hand it over to them in case they didn't approve. By now it was Sunday of week one of their new life, the house was almost settled on furniture wise bar a few minor items one being the placement of a rather different looking no let's be honest disgusting looking lamp that Amy's mother had brought them as a moving gift it was made from 3 iron flat legs that curved in then out again and housed an electric candle, yes an electric candle! In the right setting I'm sure it would fit brilliantly like a Halloween themed hotel or something but not in their new home – so it settled as extra lighting in the basement.

As the morning sun began to push through the dense branches of the vast woodland trees at the rear of their garden creating almost god like beams from above, Amy stood on the back porch a mug of coffee grasped in her hands as she gentle sipped in deep secluded thought.

"You ok hun" Max asked as he joined her, they stood in matching dressing gowns big fluffy and grey to onlookers they'd of looked like a pair of stuffed bears.

"I was just thinking about him, and how he'd of loved it out here I'm sure of it" she said referring to the child they lost at birth, it's true what they say you can move around but those things never leave you, you never escape the pains of the past you just learn to live side by side with them I guess.

"I'm sure he's looking down on us happy that we have finally took the plunge"

"Yeh, and now we can think about getting some hours in on trying again" Amy said firing a suggestive wink at Max, who in turn ushered her in the house grabbing the ass and saying

"Get up those stairs" as he did.

As the pair lay almost entangled in each other following shall we call it a heavy morning workout they dozed in and out of the Sunday morning noises, the birds chirping, trees rustling what was left of their leaves and Hank bloody Johnson with that chainsaw!

"I swear to god he uses that to cut the pissing cheese for his sandwiches" Max said slamming his fist down on the bed in frustration

"He was the one who said he liked to sleep in on Sundays!"

"I know honey but maybe we woke him up and this is payback I mean I did get a little loud" Amy said, they laughed and Max kissed her on the forehead as they cuddled.

Then came a sudden knock at the door, Max shot to his feet and flung a dressing gown on and headed downstairs, just as he got to the door he realised it was Amy's gown so he opened the door and shielded himself with it slightly. A man in a sharp suit stood there slicked back hair and a finely kept moustache

"Can I help you" Max asked.

"I am sorry to bother you on a Sunday, I am Frederick Bishop of Bishops Homes & Rentals, may I assume you are indeed Mr Jones"

"Yes, yes sir I am" Max said reaching out to shake hands

"Excuse my appearance we are catching up still from the jet lag"

"Of course, I am afraid I have some rather troubling news" Frederick Bishops bottom lip began to tremble slightly and his tone change to one of sorrow

"It's Debbie, Debbie Shultz – uhm – I was informed late last night that they – well – they found her car crashed from a cliff and that she had perished in the accident" He then began to sob slightly before regaining some slight composure

"Her body was almost completely consumed by flames, I felt you should know as I know you had seeked her out"

"Oh my god, I – I am so sorry for your loss Mr Bishop, I can't imagine how this must of effected you all, I only met her briefly but she was a lovely woman" Max said

"I owed her some money she had overseen some of the renovations for us as we weren't here and when I tried to wire the money over it failed so I wanted to get it to ..."

"Ah yes the side work" Frederick interrupted with a rather harsher tone cracking through for a moment

"I knew about that not good from her but that is of little consequence now I suppose"

"Of course I am happy to send it to her family to go towards the funeral costs"

"Yes, yes I will get the address to you once I have it, now if you will excuse me I will take my leave – good day Mr Jones"

"Good bye Mr Bishop, and thank you for coming to inform me" Max closed the door and turned around looking to the floor in bewilderment and shock.

"Christ who's died" Amy said as she sauntered down the stairs in one of Max's t-shirts swamping her.

"Debbie Shultz – car accident"

"Fuck – I was kidding, that's terrible"

"Poor woman, she never got to that family emergency and now they have to deal with death as well – could be two for all we know"

"Come here" Amy said as she stood a few steps up and rested Max's face to her chest, kissing the top of his head.

"I should let Gene know, I think they were good friends I mean she asked him to move us in" Max said.

He went to the bedroom and threw on some jeans that were crumpled up on the floor and a green t-shirt with a motorcycle on the front of it, he went into the bathroom and splashed some cold water on his face to wake him up a bit and flattened his erratic hair down. Then he wondered over to Gene who was setting ladders up to clean the ground floor windows of his home.

"Woh – Woh – Woh there fella" Stu from number 1 shouted over to Gene

"Now I've told you let me do that for ya, you have to be careful at your age Gene"

"I am perfectly capable of cleaning some bloody windows" Gene snapped back.

"I know, I know but if anything happened I wouldn't forgive myself, let me get changed and come and help" before Gene could reply Stu jogged off home to change.

As Max approached Gene he could hear him muttering what he assumed were expletives

"Have you come to tell me I'm too old to wipe my own ass or something" Gene said

"To be honest Gene I wish I was" Gene could see something was deeply troubling Max.

"What is it son, what's wrong"

"It's Debbie Shultz, she's been in an accident and has passed away – I'm sorry Gene I know you were good friends"

Gene dropped to sit on the porch steps he buried his head in his hands

"She, she was – I loved her, at a time I thought we would be together but it just didn't play out that way because of the age gap, but I never stopped loving her" he said as he began crying, Max placed a hand on his shoulder, Stu came bounding over and saw Gene crying Max gave him a shake of the head as to signal him to leave it for now which he did.

"What's happened" Alf asked as he stepped out from the house

"Gene?"

"It-its Debbie Sh-She's dead" he said battling through tears

"Oh Gene, come on let's get you inside buddy" Alf and Max lifted him up and as they went to take him in Alf stopped Max

"I will take it from here bud, thank you though for letting him know rather than reading it from some uncaring hack in the paper"

Max nodded and slowly walked off home.

He walked through the door of number 3 thinking of how a perfect week had just been wiped out with the worst of tragedies, he rubbed his eyes and sunk his head as he opened his eyes he frowned there were what looked like scratch marks faintly visible on the floor. He bent down to look closer and ran his hands over them as he did a shot of ice cold ran down his spine he let out a strange noise as he shook and dropped onto his backside, it was an uncomfortable and unnerving feeling, one like when you are in the dark at night about to get in bed and you think something will grab your legs from under it so you panic dive into bed. He heard a muffled sound as he sat in almost tunnel vision looking at the marks

"Baby" he suddenly heard with clarity, he looked up and saw Amy

"Are you ok?" she asked.

"Yeh – I – I just had a weird feeling that's all it's nothing" he jumped to his feet smiled at his wife and they walked to the kitchen, but as they did he looked back over his shoulder to the marks and an eerie cold presence consumed him again.

# CHAPTER 4:
# LADIES WHO LUNCH TOGETHER
# VACATION TOGETHER

As the summer of 1984 approached the memory of the sad events surrounding Debbie Shutz's untimely death had faded and bonds had well and truly been forged between the Jones's and their new neighbours. Stu and Max had become almost inseparable after bonding one weekend working on Stu's roof, they had ventured to the loft to do a few repairs on damaged tiles from the harsh weather autumn had brought them but a wrong step saw both men crash through the ceiling and on to the bed where the magic supposedly happens, let me tell you no magic happened for quite some time until the two men repaired the damage.

The wives had been bonding through the art of afternoon lunches, shopping trips and book clubs, today they were preparing for a weekend away at a spa a few hours' drive south and the men planned to have a barbeque out in the middle of the cul-de-sac to pound a few beers and rib each other into the early hours. Of course Hank had to perform his safety checks and had also obtained a road barrier to place at the entrance way to avoid becoming road kill, even if they were mostly the only people to ever drive there.

Hank had again declared he would be using his brand new grill that he had purchased, it still needed building but why should that stop him. Alf was the usual grill master but the guys had told him and Gene to relax and let the young cubs take care of it all which they begrudgingly agreed to, they along with Dennis, Stu and Max gathered on Hanks porch with some bottles of beer watching on as the grill master built his new toy down on the grass adjacent to the pavement. The men sniggered and offered their help as Hank fumbled along with beads of sweat rolling down his cheeks in the mid morning sun

"No – no don't you worry fellas I've got this" he would say each time they offered

"Ta-da" he said holding his hands out presenting the newly erected grill like a game show hostess revealing the prizes. All five men burst into hysterics

"What" he asked.

"Hank – you have – you have put the grill on backwards" Max said before erupting into laughter again. Hank stood and looked for a second, he had indeed put the top on backwards the doors underneath were on front and the controls and opening to the grill itself on the back, Hank kicked the box it had been packed in across the grass expletives spewing from his mouth.

"Don't worry pal, we will help you switch it around" Dennis said as he put a reassuring hand on Hanks shoulder, Gene and Alf gave each other a look that screamed – *this wouldn't of happened if we'd of been in charge!* While the men dismantled the barbeque Amy Jones, Jenny Patterson, Cara Thompson and the long suffering Martha Johnson were packing bags into Cara's black 1974 Ford Ranch Wagon, It had belonged to her father before his passing in 82' from pancreatic cancer. The residents always commented on how immaculate it was kept, Cara would wash and polish it an every given opportunity as it was all she had left to remind her of the father she idolised.

The ladies were only going for a two night stay at Belle Vue Spa & Hotel but they seemed to be carrying enough luggage to see them through a month or so.

"Do you have the shoe bag Jenny?" Cara asked as she pummelled a small white bag into a tiny gap in the bottom corner of the boot space.

"It's on the back seat we don't want them damaged now do we" Jenny said.
Martha was sat in the car patiently waiting for the others to check, check and then check again on the exact same bags to ensure they had every essential they would require, she opened the shoe bag in which all the ladies had piled shoes for any situation into and took a peek, on the top sat a pair of gleaming red shoes that Cara had brought several months ago but never gotten around to wearing. The women were unaware but they were the very same shoes Debbie Shultz passed and one day hoped to buy as a treat for a successful job done with the Jones's.

"Right come kiss your wives goodbye boys before we leave and get swept up by millionaires" Amy shouted to the men who had now managed to resolve the backwards barbeque issue, even Hank was laughing about it, probably more to hide the immense embarrassment than the fact he found it amusing. As the couples bid farewell to each other Martha had gotten out from the back of the car and was instructing Hank on how to cope without her for a couple of nights

"Now there are sandwiches in the fridge, labelled up for you, I have brought some of those microwavable meals as you know you don't do well with the stove" Hank who looked as if he had the demeanour of a 7 year old being lectured by his mother nodded intently

"And under no circumstances try to wash your dirty clothes – no matter how mucky you get" she said referring to last November when the snows came and Hank flooded the basement it was so cold down there it was almost like an indoor ice rink.

Max stood with his hand on Amy's cheek, as they gazed into each other's eyes

"Will you tell them this weekend" he said.

"Yeh I think it's safe to tell them now, I will wait until after we call to let you all know we have arrived safe"

"I will do the same" They smiled and kissed each other goodbye, it was a proud day for Max as he got to tell the fellas he was to be a father. They had found out 3 months previous but due to losing their first child at birth they didn't want to tempt fate by announcing things early.

The car ladened with women, clothes, and shoes drove away up the slope exiting Vernon's Place then disappeared right onto Pontins Street

"Let's drink BEER!" Dennis erupted and the guys all cheered, Gene and Alf began to drag out a cooler filled to bursting point with beers.

"Damn it you two y'all put your backs out let us get that" Dennis said as he and Stu ushered the pair out the way and brought the beers to the middle of the sac.

"Incapable of carrying things now too Alfie" Gene said as the two stood watching the young cubs as they referred to them swilling beers about and nattering like old hens at the grill.

"If only they knew what we have achieved" Alf said.

"They wouldn't believe it if we told them bud" the two clinked bottles and went to join the others. Not too much was really known about Alf and Gene other than they basically built the houses around them they had been there so long, and that they had both served in the military but they rarely spoke of it and when they did it was in little detail.

The evening cascaded into copious amounts of beer being drank and spilt, amazing food cooked to military perfection by Hank on his new grill which he showed off with the pride of a new father bringing his child home for the first time and singing which many would liken to the last wale of a dying animal, Stu had not long staggered out from a 20 minute phone call from Jenny informing them they had arrived safely apart from and I quote 'The blind coffin dodgers' who nearly collided with them on the freeway.

"Shhh – hush – shhhhh" a well oiled Max rose to his feet clinking a small spoon to his bottle of half drunken beer

"I have an impotent – I mean important thing to say"
Hank stood to up and ushered silence to the others.

"I am proud to announce that I am having a baby"

"Jesus mate have your waters broke" Stu yelled through fits of laughter.

"N-N-No I can't have a baby I have a penis" Max sniggered

"I mean Amy is pregnant"

Cheers echoed around the darkening street, hugs were shared as bottles clinked and handshakes were exchanged with Dennis's small battery powered radio the cassette player held shut with some tape, and a wire hanger in place of the aerial rumbled on in the background with Reg Venus's Golden hour playing songs from the 60's and 70's. The winds had begun to pick up and napkins, paper plates and wrappers were now dancing around the cul-de-sac almost rhythmically to Staying Alive. It had been on the news earlier in the day that the tail end of a storm may hit them over the weekend but they were well into the alcohol supplies by then and decided it was worth the risk.

A flash of light flickered in the distance past the trees to the back of the houses and after a few moments later a faint rumbling sound

"We best get this stuff in out the way" Gene said. The men hurried all be it rather comically as they stumbled and staggered around trying to collect items now rolling and flapping around in the wind, Max chasing a beer bottle around the curve of the sac. Hank who had drank a good amount himself seemed the most alert of the group other than Gene and Alf who drank much less than the others had taken charge of the knives and other dangerous items to avoid accidents in the rush. The men sheltered on the porch of number 3 as rain started to lash down putting a stop to several napkins that had been fluttering around as the water melted them to the road.

"I am making a dash for home" Hank said

"I have plenty of wood in the garage I need to chop up ready for the winter, have to prepare"

"You've been drinking man you will do yourself a mischief" Alf said.

"Me? Not likely old timer, takes more than a few beers to get me wobbly I can tell you" he pulled his shirt up over his head revealing the his stomach hanging over his jeans filled with hotdogs, burgers and beer, I want to say he shuffled but I really can't describe exactly how Hank moved at a speed faster than walking but one thing they all noticed was he was swaying a little.

"We should really stop him chopping wood guys" Max said.

"Ah, he will be fine he always puts safety first remember" Gene replied.

The men dispersed to their homes, closing up storm shutters on the outsides of their respective properties, some like Dennis putting towels at the foot of the door to soak up and wayward rain, Hank hooking a small generator up to the fridge in the garage in case they lose power. He then proceeded to uncover a large stack of logs that was at least 4 feet high piled against the far wall of his garage, he got out his beloved petrol chainsaw which despite much use looked brand new due to Hank adoringly cleaning it from top to bottom after every use. Hank treated everything he owned no matter how big or small with the upmost care, everything could be mistaken for brand new even his grandfathers old clock which stood proudly in his lobby not a mark on it, it had been passed through the family for years and one day Hank would pass it to his daughter Bernadette. He opened the garage door to help filter out the fumes that the chainsaw would make and took the can of Premium Chainsaw Oil from his top shelf removed the lid took a quick sniff of it as he always did – he seemed to enjoy the scent, placed a funnel in the tank and began to cautiously top it up so to not spill any.

He placed the chainsaw on the floor grasped the starter and tugged powerfully, it spluttered and shook a little before falling dormant, again he tugged forcefully with the same reaction a third and fourth attempts also ended in nothing however at the fifth time of asking the saw rumbled into life juddering away as the chain moved slickly along its runner as thunder and lightning began to flash and clatter in the darkened night sky onlookers who didn't know him would think Hank looked like some mad deranged killer from a horror movie.

As Hank began to chop his way through a small forests worth of wood, Max cranked the volume of his record player up to dull the screams of metal on wood Queens 1977 News Of The World battled the screams with Sheer Heart Attack powering away from the speakers, meanwhile Dennis was turning the volume dial up to continue watching a rerun of Miami Vice as he never normally got to watch it due to Cara having strange distain for Don Johnson I think it was to do with him being divorced from Melanie Griffith who she adored – but that was never confirmed to my knowledge. Stu who could sleep through pretty much anything had passed out on his sofa with some god awful Z list horror movie on the box, As Alf and Gene sat at the kitchen table drinking coco and shooting the breeze about the night and what they planned to do now the festivities were cut short.

After about an hour of firewood cutting Hank now soaked more so than if he had stood out in the rain from sweat, his arms aching and shaking to the core from the juddering chainsaw decided a break for refreshment was in order so he sat the saw still running down on the ground and headed to the kitchen. He swilled out an empty glass from earlier and filled it with water which he gulped down at haste, he then downed another glass before filling it a third time but this time sipping gently as he mopped how brow with a kitchen towel and regained his breath a little. He then heard a clanging noise from the garage one akin to a tool dropping to the floor.

Hank stepped out into the garage

"Hello – Max is that you" he said looking around the empty space, he spotted a small wrench on the floor which he supposed had fallen off its hook somehow and returned it he rested his glass on the shelf as he did so he heard what sounded like a chair scuff across the kitchen floor *I bet it's that bloody cat* he thought, all the residents on Vernon's had been pestered by the fat ginger tomcat they believed lived somewhere on Pontins Street. He stormed in for some reason barking like a dog I assume hoping to frighten the cat out, but there was nothing total silence until from the lounge he heard the TV click on the closing music from Miami Vice sounding off, he gulped nervously as his body felt like it was flipping within itself, his skin crawling with dread

"Who – Who's there" he said slowly stepping forwards as he reached for a rolling pin on the kitchen table, then as he felt all the hairs on the back of his neck stand to attention a whisper shocked his ears

"Hank" it said, he spun around on the spot a quick glance of a masked figure engulfed his vision before his world fell into darkness.

# CHAPTER 5:
# THE EVER RUNNING MOUTH OF HANK JOHNSON

Hanks eyes opened with a sharp intake of breath as the faint sound of his chainsaw chugged gently in the background, a pain throbbed from his forehead as his blurry vision began to correct itself. He noticed his back felt uncomfortable it soon became clear it was his  arms tied behind his back, he tried to move his legs but they also had been tied together, so tight in fact that the bulging skin of his shins was going a shade of purple. As he gazed in trance like confusion at the kitchen ceiling a man who looked to his foggy eyes to be pure black shadow appeared with two piercing eyes fixed on him from above, he took a deep intake of breath and just as he prepared to yell with all he had for help the man smashed a fist across Hanks face blood sprayed the walls making a sound almost like rain on plastic and the rattle of two teeth hitting chairs and the floor was followed by the faint breathy crying of poor helpless Hank Johnson.

"Not clever Hanky panky, not clever at all" the man said pacing back and forth looking down on his victim

"Try again and I relieve you of your tongue"
Hank trembling with fear nodded.

"Good man" the man slapped Hank on the
cheek a couple of times.

"My oh my Hanky, the founding member and
leader of the Residents Association – what a fine job
you have done protecting the people of this burb with
your incessant nagging, continual curtain twitching
you really have done a fine job" the man began a slow
arrogantly patronising clap.

"But you missed something, and it was a
doozy! You see, you kinda missed when I sliced that
fucking bitch Debbie Shultz head off"
With a sudden rush of confidence Hank raised his
head slightly

"Y-You couldn't have, she – she died in a car
accident" he said, a slight slur accounted to the pain
of losing some teeth.

"Oh yeh the dipshit Police here lapped that
up, anything for an easy open and closed case for the
donut brigade" the man pulled a chair up and
straddled it the back facing towards Hank who until
now hadn't really realised he was lay on the kitchen
table.

"It was easy, I sliced her throat tidied her up
waited until I saw your drooling ass asleep slumped in
the chair by the window took her and her car on a
little drive and sent them off a cliff – Bingo bitch
gone" the man said.

 He stood up sliding the chair away from the
table.

"Ah shit – I went and told you didn't I, I
fucking told you! Jesus you are good at getting info
out of people and all you did was sob and lose a

couple of teeth"

"I w-w-won't tell anyone I swear, I have money you can take it and go I won't tell them anything" Hanks said

"Oh Hanky, there are two problems with you my man, both are to do with your mouth"
The man was rummaging through what appeared to be one of Hanks bags from the garage.

"You see one thing about you is you never know when to shut the fuck up"

"I do, I will I..."

"Shut Up!" the man smashed his fist onto the table

"You see you yammer on even when you know you shouldn't, it's a bad habit – ah ha" the man removed a small flimsy box from the bag and from that he removed some hemming web tape, he then walked over to the corner of the kitchen where the ironing board sat, picked up the iron and plugged it in over by the table.

Hank started to talk rambling begging pleading it was pretty much inaudible he was starting to fidget until a white light flashed in front of his eyes and his ears felt muffled, as his sight began to return he could see two of the man in black stood looking at him he clenched his eyes tightly shut for a few seconds and then opened them and the man was stood there and it was back to one of them.

"I haven't headbutted anyone in a while felt fucking fantastic for me, I dare say not so much for you" the man said a hint of glee in his voice

"Anyway as you can't be trusted you leave me no choice" he then slapped a cutting of the hemming web over Hanks mouth followed by several more to create a thick tight layer.

"So as I was saying Hanky boy, the first of your problems is you can't shut up and you have demonstrated this very well tonight for me. But fear not I am here to help" with that the man grabbed a chunk of Hanks hair tightly and held his head down firm on the table, Hank trying desperately to reason with him and beg through muffled mumbles. Then to his terror the man brought the iron into his vision before Hank had chance to react he pushed to his mouth, Hanks body went stiff as muffled screams cried from beneath the cloud of steam, the smell of burning glue and flesh began to fill the air

"Fuck me Hanky that shit stinks"
You could hear the sizzling and blistering of the skin as it melted into the webbing and vice versa. Another scent caught the man's attention and he looked down to see Hank had pissed himself, as he pulled the iron away some skin had fused to it and it slowly tore away almost Velcro sounding as it did.

Hanks mouth was now red raw, blistered and oozing with blood, snot bubbling from his nose tears streamed from his eyes down to pool in the creases of his ears before dribbling to the table. His eyes were rolling around in their sockets he was on the verge of passing out from the excruciating pain, his world went dark for a moment until an ice cold, sharp pain shocked him back to consciousness in the form of a glass of water thrown over his face.

"No Hanky you can't go just yet buddy, we have more to work on – remember there were two issues caused by that mouth of yours" the man walked off into the garage, Hank tried to poke his lips with his tongue from the inside but the pain of even thinking about it was way too much.

"Hold these would ya" the man said tossing two large hooks on to Hanks chest, he then proceeded the tie a rope to one of the beams that ran across the kitchen ceiling

"So in a way we have solved both problems sealing that trap of yours, as problem number 2 is you don't stop fucking eating either do ya" the man checked the rope was secure by tugging at it a little uttering

"It'll do" to himself.

"I mean we have stopped you eating so much going forwards, but I want to help you lose that hanging gut Hanky and fast! so I have a plan, you'll love it"

Instantly Hanks inner monologue was telling him how much he probably wouldn't like it. The man grabbed Hanks large hanging stomach and held it up as much as he could then smashed the ends of the two hooks through the large excess skin, again Hanks body tightened and he writhed a little but that tore his skin more, he froze as the man connected the hooks to the rope thus suspending his large gut upright.

"You know what they say Hanky no pain, no gain buddy"

Little did the other residents know as they slept off the beers, listened to music, watched films and took in the 11 o'clock news that behind all the noise outside which occasionally included the screams of a chainsaw on wood that the man who had watched them all these years was in a state of sheer terror, he needed the help this time but they had become so intent on blocking out the noise and in a way Hank himself that they had left him suffering alone.

"The thing I love about weight loss Hank is you can do it in your own home, using your very own equipment" the man said as he again vanished to the garage as he returned the grumble of the chainsaw seemed to get louder, dread then flushed over Hank his breathing heightened bubbling snot popped from his nose under the melted skin and webbing you could not mistake the muffled cries of '*No No*'.

The man stood over him and winked, he then grasped the ignition and the blades began to churn as he thrust the chainsaw against the suspended gut squelching, tearing and splutters off cuts of skin everywhere, blood sprayed like a sprinkler system all over the kitchen. Hank convulsing through the shock and trauma until with what sounded like the tearing of a fabric shirt the body weight severed the gut from the body and organs began to spill out. The man leaned over Hank whose life was leaving his body rapidly

"You're welcome" he said as he removed his mask, Hank realised the man was someone he knew, a friend. He turned his head to the side and in his final moments he didn't think of the pain as by now his body had forgotten how to feel it, nor the revelation of his killer he thought of Martha, dear sweet long suffering Martha.

As Max stirred having dozed off listening to Queen in his armchair he noticed rather oddly everything was switched off, he glanced at his watch it was 12:13am so he had been out for a few hours. He yawned and rubbed his eyes as he stood up and flicked the light switch – nothing, he tried the TV, a lamp and even opened the fridge all fruitless. He looked out to the street but all of the street lights were off he couldn't see any hint of a street light for quite some distance from the window at least. Max began to focus on the entrance to the cul-de-sac it looked as if something was covering it but he couldn't quite make it out through the rain and darkness, he moved his head closer to the window and tried to focus harder – Bang – a hand hit the window

"Open up man" Stu who resembled a drowned rat said from outside. Max opened the door and Stu dripped his way in.

"The power is totally out man" Stu said.

"We should call the station see how long for, freaks the shit outta me being in the dark alone"

"I will call them I have the number in our book" Max said as he picked up a small yellow book which was like an encyclopaedia of telephone numbers all written out neatly by Amy every letter 'i' topped with a love heart

"Here it is" Max lifted the handset off the phone and dialled the number, but as he lifted the handset to his ear a look of frowned confusion covered his face,

"It's dead"

"What do you mean its dead?"

"The phone lines, they must be down as well" he put the phone down and headed to the window

"I swear there is something over there on the road, we should check it out, it may be what's causing it" Max grabbed his flashlight from the draw and threw a raincoat on while hilariously throwing Stu Amy's bright pink one to wear! They then headed out into the unrelenting rain.

"Hey fellas wait up" Gene shouted as he

headed over to Max and Stu

"Your phones dead too?"

"Yeh complete silence, we are heading towards Pontins to see what's happening and check if there is anything visibly causing it – I think I saw something on the road"

"I will tag along, I left Alf with the phone so he can keep trying it" Gene said as the three men walked along the slick wet road glimmering with the flickers of moonlight sneaking through gaps in the clouds. The torch light caught the shape of something as the men approached closer, trees two of the gigantic thick Oakwood trees had come down in the storm and taken both the power and phone lines with them.

"Must of been the lightening that hit'em" Stu said

"Would of taken one hell of a strike to move these things I mean the entire road is now blocked off" Max said. He then walked towards the stump of the tree

"Holy shit"

"What" Gene asked rushing over.

"It wasn't lightening that struck these trees, they were cut down" the men all looked at the stump which was indeed cleanly cut with no scorch marks as one would expect to see from a lightning strike.

"Why would someone – I mean surely we would of heard it" Stu said

"I had my music on loud to drown out ..." Max froze "– to drown out Hank chopping wood"

"Do you think that dumb fucker did this?"

"There's only one way to find out" Gene said as he looked towards Hanks house which was now all closed up and in darkness.

"Maybe he was drunker than he thought and just started chopping trees down, I mean this is Hank we are talking about here"

"Stu's right he wouldn't do this on purpose, surely?" Max said.

Gene looked at the two men.

"You never know what's going on in people's minds really especially his!"

"What the hell you fellas doing out here in the rain some sort of circle jerk?" Dennis asked as he splashed his way over.

"The fucks with the trees?"

"It appears the Residents Association Leader chopped them down while pissed and now the power and phone lines are out" Stu said.

"Fuck sake the dumb bastard – Hank you dumb shit what you done" Dennis shouted towards number 4. The four men headed over, their shoes squelching across the grass borders of the pavements.

"He's probably embarrassed or passed out on the sofa so let's not go mad at him guys – ok" Max said as the others begrudgingly nodded in agreement. He hammered his fist on the door and it creeped open.

"Hank – you in here buddy" he said but silence was his only reply, he looked to the men behind as he opened the door and began to step in completely oblivious to the horrific scene they were about to encounter.

# CHAPTER 6:
## YOU CANNOT LEAVE

The floor creaked gently as the four men entered the lobby, the ticking of Hank's Grandfathers clock relentless in the background. All the curtains had been closed so the flashlight was all they had and it was dimming the batteries draining of life.

"Turn it off its pretty useless now Max" Dennis said, Max put the torch down on a table in the lobby that he had stumbled across while fumbling around.

"Hank you idiot wake up" Dennis shouted.

"Man shut up leave the poor guy alone" Max said as he opened the curtains in the lounge to let a little of the natural night light in.

The men led by Max walked slowly towards the kitchen, a squelching sound came from under Max's foot as he stepped closer , he took another step and slipped crashing onto his back as he did he felt sprays of what he assumed was water.

"Ah man that's brilliant" Stu laughed
Dennis stepped with care on the slippery tiled floor to the window.

"The stupid ass clown has flooded his fucking house I tell you he should be put in the loony bin" he yanked the curtains open the moon had broken through a gap in the clouds and shone perfectly towards the kitchen window of number 4 and in the moon lit room the men were greeted with the most horrific of sites.

Hanging from the ceiling a large clump of flesh dripping with blood and guts, Hanks body wide open guts dribbling to the floor, the walls sprayed and with blood, skin and fat. Stu slid like baby deer on ice to the sink and proceeded to throw up.

"Oh fuck – oh shit – oh fuckery shit fuck shit" Dennis said as he turned and ran towards the front door, Max lay in a pool of blood and guts that moments before he assumed was water in complete shock tears streaming down his face, Gene grabbed Stu by the collar and Max by the arm

"Come on fellas we have to get out" he said. The four men skidded and slid across the floor, blood coating their shoes. Once outside they fell to the floor with tears and mass panic engulfing them as blood began to wash from Max's clothes as he lay in the road almost motionless with shock.

"Alf!" Gene shouted and began running towards number 5.

"Gene wait" Max said

"I will be fine just wait here"
The men sat soaked to the bone just looking towards number 5 for what felt like hours, 10 minutes passed

"I'm going in" Max raised to his feet, just then a figure staggered from the house, the men looked on as Gene came into focus a look of shear despair etched on his face.

"He's – He's dead" Gene fell to the floor, Max went to go in to the house

"Leave him Max, I have covered him. Leave

him at peace".

Max nodded and sat besides Gene putting an arm around his shoulder as Gene watched his tears drop from his eyes and wash away in the midnight rain.

"We have to get the fuck outta here" Stu said shooting up to his feet.

"There is some mad fuck probably escaped from some nutters hospital cutting folks up, well I for one aint sticking around! I am climbing over them fucking trees and getting the fuck out of here" He was twitching like a junky in need of a fix, his nerves in overdrive he ran over and began to climb the trees. He got halfway up then a snapping noise echoed around the sac and Stu cried out in agony, slamming his hands on the trunks of the trees writhing around drool and snot streaming from his face. The others raced over Dennis snapped a thin branch away which was obscuring their vision to reveal a bear trap had gripped onto Stu's ankle the teeth had torn straight through it his Achilles sliced in two blood squirted from his leg as he shook breathing erratically.

"Jesus fucking Christ" Max yelled

"I – I Have a crowbar at home let me grab it we can try prise it open" he ran off into the darkness. The minutes ticked away

"W – W – Where – Where is he" Stu sobbed propped against the trunk of one of the trees, he was desperate to lay down but the angle would of been excruciating for him.

"Fuck it" Dennis said

"I'm getting Hanks" he headed to Hanks garage and pulled the door open a small light flicked on, Hank often had small generators or battery lights in case the power went out, Dennis stopped for a second as he could see blood slowly leaking down the steps into the garage from under the Kitchen entrance. He spotted a large metal bar and took it over to Stu, he wedged it in the small gap left where the leg bone was holding the trap a jar

"This isn't going to be nice fella, bite on this" Dennis passed Stu a small wooden branch

"On 3, 1 – 2 –" He pulled and the trap open blood oozed out and the distinct 'shling' sound of metal brushing past something could be heard, but no screams no sounds of any kind from Stu he didn't even move bar one solitary flinch, the branch he was biting on fell to the floor and the men looked up and almost as one gasped in fear, Stu was motionless with a large hunting knife exiting his mouth it then yanked upwards powerfully until it sliced through the top of his head – blood and brains glooped out and his body crumbled in a heap, A man stood all in black atop the trees a large blade grasped in his hand blood and bits of skull drooling from it, his piercing eyes fixed on them

"You cannot leave, there are traps like this everywhere, and I have insurances you try to go anywhere and I start killing these insurances – I'm always watching you so just play the game by the rules" he growled before the knife and his eyes vanished into the rustling of the braches which soon faded. Dennis and Gene stood trembling, shock coursing through them like electricity, Dennis gripping the metal bar in front of him like a baseball bat.

"Jesus couldn't find this for looking" Max said as he re-appeared crowbar in hand, the two men spun around Dennis pointing the bar towards him

"Whoa – what the fuck man"

"You took your time" Dennis said.

"Yeh I said I couldn't find it, what the hell is wro – how's Stu? Why can't I hear him – Stu you ok?"

"He's fucking dead his head in split in two, but how do we know you didn't already know that? I mean you vanished he died – the killer vanished a couple of minutes later you pop up"

"What the fuck are you on, I would never ever even consider something like that you ginger prick – now let me see him" Max stepped forwards and was struck with a hefty thud across the face with the bar. His crowbar flew from his hands and clattered across the road a sharp stinging sensation throbbed across his left cheek, his eyes seemed foggy.

"Give me that you idiot" Gene ripped the bar from Dennis's hands

"Are you insane? Not happy with a psycho slaughtering us one by one but you now want us to turn on each other?"

"No – you have to admit timing is real dodgy"

"Maybe but we know this man, and after all you weren't accounted for when Hank died – in fact none of us were so do we assume everyone is guilty?"

"No – hey Max I'm so –" Dennis was suddenly on his ass, Max had recovered enough to swing a right hook at his jaw.

"Apology accepted, we need to get safe"

"Let's go to mine I have some candles and a first aid kit for your face" Dennis said picking himself up

"Why what's wrong with it?"

"You have a little scratch that's all"

but by little scratch Dennis referred to a gash that was pretty deep from the hit he took off the bar.

The men cautiously entered number 2 via the rear entrance with Dennis gripping the bar, Gene and Max picked up knives as they came through the kitchen locking doors behind them as they went. They secured the house and set about lighting it up with candles, Cara had put some seriously thick curtains up so no light would escape with them shut, the others often thought they were out as the house appeared in darkness when in fact it was the curtain doing a fine job. Gene began to clean up Max's cut

"This will need stitches kid"

"That's the least of our worries, why they hell is this happening to us" Max said.

"I dunno sometimes these people just go loopy, or in some cases it like a drug to them. I remember years ago when me and Alf were in the military, there was these two guys they would move around small towns slaughtering people. They got caught once by this young cop he had them in his squad car after a routine check and was waiting for back up, he asked them why they did what they did – their answer was it's a game for us a sport! I mean what kinda sick madmen must they of been!"

"What happened to them?"

"Well when the backup arrived they found the young cop without his eyes at the side of his car, no idea how they got free. After that pretty sure they retired maybe getting caught put them off who knows" Gene put some gauze and medical tape on Max's face and they shared an appreciative nod. Dennis then fumbled in with some snacks

"I got chips or crisps as you Brits call'em, you

weirdo's" he smiled, it was clear he felt bad for his moment of panic and accusation towards Max.

"Thanks ginge" The men sat on the lounge floor in silence munching on the chips and sipping some lukewarm beer that had been in the fridge, now wasn't really the time for beer but it also felt like the best time for it, tears began to drip to the floor as Dennis sniffled.

"They were good people all of'em Hank, Stu and Alf to a man they didn't deserve this"

"No one deserves this" Max said and the three men clinked their bottles.

"To our friends" Gene whispered and the three men repeated,

"To our friends" followed by a slow sip of beer.

"We need to try and get some rest"

"Yeh Gene's right, we don't know if they are gone or how long we have until they return, Dennis you two put your heads down for an hour or so I will keep watch"

"Nah man you rest I was out of it for hours earlier I'll be fine"

"If you're sure – thanks" Max patted Dennis on the shoulder and lay down, he looked to the ceiling and closed his eyes but all he saw was flashes of Hanks mutilated body and blood – *sleep huh, good luck with that* – he thought. He tried to concentrate on something far more important Amy and his new bun in the oven, he closed his eyes for a moment, when he opened them he was in a small windowless padded room with a single light bulb flickering dimly above him, he tried to move his arms but looked down to see he was confined to a straight jacket. As he looked frantically around the room a shadow in the far corner caught his eye

"Hello" he asked there was no reply instead a high pitched sobbing sound.

"Who are you, where am I? Did everyone get out ok?"

The sobbing continued for a moment

"Daddy –" the voice of a small boy whimpered from the corner

"Look what you made happen Daddy" it said sobbing and whining.

"I'm sorry kid, I'm not your Dad" The shadow appeared to spin around and with a sinister screeching voiced screamed

"Yes you are Maxwell, yes you are" the light brightened slightly and Max scurried back up to the corner furthest away from the boy. As the child stepped forwards more into the light he was all skin and bone, just a large filthy torn t-shirt for clothes his eyes were black holes blood streaming from them and the boys toe and fingernails appeared to of been ripped from his hands and feet.

"My god what happened to you – what happened to you" Max said

"You left us – you left us – you left us" the boy started repeating over and over again as he lurched across the room reaching out with both hands

"You left us – you left us – you ..." he stopped dead and the lights went out, Max's heavy panicked breathing was all that could be heard then the lights shone bright and the child was right in his face

"LEFT US!" he screamed jumping on Max choking him

"MAX – MAX – MAX" the boy screamed, then with a jolt Max awoke on the floor of number 2

"Max, wake up mate come look"

He took a moment to gather himself and then went to the window he peeped through a small gap in the curtains there was a flashlight in his house, a dim one but definitely a flash light.

"You still think it was me ginge" he said.

"No, no I fucking well don't".

# CHAPTER 7:
# THE 3AM GUN RUN

The three men watched fixated as the dim light fluttered around the rooms of number 3, after all as long as he was in there he wasn't coming for them – however trying to run would be difficult if there were more traps by the fallen trees and the chances of being spotted were high.

"We could go out the back through the woods and onto Pontins that way" Dennis said

"We can't risk even the slightest chance that he hasn't set stuff up in the woods fellas, besides we try to leave and he will use those insurances he spoke of, god knows what they are! Or just as bad he gets away free to do this to others or worse come back for you and your wives"

"Gene's right" Max said stepping away from the windows and perching on the edge of an armchair

"We have to try stopping him, there are three of us and one of him. Does either of you have a gun?"

"No, me and Alf swore never again after we left the military"

"I don't but Stu has his Dads old hunting rifle, he was storing it for him"

"Do you know where it is?"

"Last I saw it was in his office, in the cabinet and the bullets too I think" Dennis said, he sat in deep thought for a moment and shook his head

"Fuck sake, we have no choice – I will go I know exactly where it should be"

"You can't go alone" Max said

"I have to, it will be easier to try and stay unseen" Dennis then gestured to wait a moment and headed upstairs, he returned moments later with two small battery powered walkie talkies, The others looked at him with somewhat questionable expressions

"They are Cara's nephew's for when he stays he likes to play soldier in the woods, ok?!"

"Aww I'm sure Uncy Dennis does too" Max teased.

The men tested the walkies, though they weren't sure how well they would cope with the weather, but Stu lived at number 1 so at least the distance wasn't too bad.

"If we see that bastard we will alert you straight away should give you time to get out the back, if this happens come to the back door tap twice on the glass and once on the wood that way we know it's definitely you" Gene said as he passed Dennis a black pair of gloves off the side, they decided to learn from their enemy and dress Dennis as dark as possible under the left arm of his jacket cuff they strapped a white tape around it so they would know it was him if in doubt.

"You get in any trouble you let us know however you can"

"Sure thing Max, believe me you'll fucking know" Dennis laughed with a nervous shaken tone and headed out the back door which was then gently locked behind him. *Oh yeh Dennis let's run around in the pitch black while some stab happy bastard is on the loose brilliant idea* – he thought as he carefully stepped down the side of his house, it reminded him of how he would creep in the bedroom at 2am after promising to home around 11, he picked up a couple of small random branches the wind had relieved the trees of. First he had to obtain Stu's keys thus eliminating the need to smash glass or doors to get in, unfortunately that meant climbing on the fallen trees which may be set up with more traps so he planned to throw some branches down as he goes and if the snap comes run like a man possessed back to the house.

He crept along slow and low being watched by Max and Gene from the windows, they had now blown out the candles as a precaution in case any light escaped the curtain gaps. Every now and then he would glance towards number 3 to check the dim light was still visible which it was – *what is that fucker doing in there* – he thought as he reached the trees, he got as low as possible and began to almost slither across the coarse bark, the sudden clatter of a trash can clanged in the distance he slumped flat and peeked towards the house the light had moved closer to the window but he couldn't see anyone looking – *must have been a cat* – he thought. He took a deep long breath and continued slowly, as he went to lift himself to get closer to Stu's blood and rain soaked corpse slumped on top of the tree pile he felt a slight scratch on the side of his hand, he tried to pull it away but it was caught – on a large 9 inch nail he looked around him and noticed several others had been placed on wood, yet more traps to stop them leaving that way.

Dennis carefully positioned himself removed the glove from his right hand and reached into Stu's pocket he found the keys and pulled them out slowly in a tight grasp to avoid jangling them

"Thanks man" he whispered to Stu's lifeless body as he began to slowly make his way off the trees.

"He's got them" Gene said as he watched on intently

"The light is still upstairs from what I can tell"

"Yeh hallway seems dimly lit so must be in the bedroom, what the fuck is he up to"

"Probably searching the house for you or all of us, a top to bottom sort of search you know?"

"I swear to god Gene I am going to find out why the hell this fucker is doing this even if it kills me"

"Let's hope it doesn't come to that son" Gene watched as Dennis edged on.

As he approached the back door he noticed it was ajar, he knelt behind a small bush to obscure the view of his position from the back yards

"Can you guys hear me" he whispered gently over the walkie talkie, it crackled for a moment

"Yeh its Max what's wrong?"

"The back door is open, I repeat the back door is fucking open" he tensed his hand up in frustration ready to punch the life out of the mushy grass below, he then cricked his neck "Is the light still visible in number 3"

"Yes but it's too risky come back here"

"I can't we need this fucking gun – watch that light like a fucking hawk I'm going in stay quiet unless something happens it's 3am now if I aint out in 15 minutes you have to make a run for the woods end of, now do not reply to this" he reached behind to slide the walkie in to his back pocket and headed into the house.

There was an eerie cold chill about the place the sort that makes your spine shudder, maybe because it was now the home of a man murdered just feet away or maybe because of the intense feeling of being in such a situation inside a pitch black house either was a justifiable reason. Dennis looked into the lounge to see if by some spark of luck the gun had been put in there maybe while being cleaned but as he focused straining his eyes in the darkness there was no sign of it just the shadow of the coat stand in the corner, a few magazines on the table and a half drank bottle of beer on the floor next to the sofa. *Wonderful let's go upstairs while the maniac is on the loose that always goes well* - he thought as he placed his foot carefully on the bottom step a deep clunking noise greeted it as the wood which had risen slightly over time pressed back down rubbing the nails holding it in place, no matter how gently he placed his weight there were creaks and groans from the steps as he climbed them one by one. As he reached the landing he looked through the side window over to number 3 he could see the light much better looking at the front of the house as appose to the side like Max and Gene, it was brightly gleaming in the front bedroom which gave him a sense of peace about the situation. 8 minutes had passed since radio silence as Gene called it began, Max watched number 3 wondering why the man had spent so long in his house, at that moment the landing lit up

"Gene, I think he's leaving looks like he's on the stairs – let Dennis know"

"Hang on let's see where he goes, Dennis has time. You watch out the front I will watch the back" The two watched on then Max noticed the light shine out onto the road.

"Gene, he's out the fr ..." he fell silent his breath deepening,

"What is it son"

"The torch is attached to a fucking cat!"Max said watching the tomcat saunter off.

"Dennis get the hell out of there" Gene whispered over the radio

"Dennis – Dennis I repeat get the hell out the torch was on a cat" but there was no reply.

Dennis opened the door to the office slowly, it creaked a little as it widened he stepped slowly into the room which had a large oak desk in front of a window one of those god awful wooden roller chairs that made your ass forget it existed it went so numb. On the left hand wall there was a large glass front cabinet with trophies from high school and college, a picture of Stu a tall lanky streak with jet black hair holding his employee of the year award at work, sure it was only a supermarket but he lived for doing a great job there. There were other valuable life mementos such as a manky old boot which was the first thing Stu ever caught on a fishing trip with his dad, but there was a large gap where the gun should be, Dennis's heart sank. Suddenly he heard a faint scuff noise from downstairs he waited for a moment but heard nothing else, as he reached for the walkie talkie his rear pocket felt a little flat, he grasp at it

"Fuck" he yelped, it wasn't there – *I must of missed my fucking pocket by the bushes* – he thought now frantically looking around no idea what to do. For some reason his mind wondered to thinking about the lounge in particular the coat stand in the corner

"Stu doesn't have a coat stand" he said as his stomach flipped and churned.

A black shape crashed through the door of the office, knocking Dennis to the ground. He tried to get up but he felt the thud of a boot to the ribs he collapsed wincing for air, he rolled onto his back and a boot crunched down on to his nose shattering it in half bone ripped through his skin as blooded exploded from his face the man in black knelt over him and grabbed his throat tightly.

"This pains me Dennis because I wanted to really spend some time with you" he said clenching tighter, Dennis clawed at the man's arms to get him to stop but he soon grew weaker and his arms slipped away.

"Shame you won't get to see who I am like the others have and will, so I will just ..."
At that moment blood sprayed from the man's mouth he fell to the side screaming in pain, Dennis's arm in the air holding a blood soaked pen knife.

"Dennis!" Max shouted from downstairs, the man in black jumped to his feet and ran out the room the sound of a smashing window soon followed. Gene came into the room

"Jesus Dennis what the hell happened".

"You should see the other guy" Dennis said as he coughed and tried to catch his breath.

"He got out the back window off the porch roof" Max said as he came in.

"I cut the cunt, he's hurt" Dennis said
"But the guns gone I'm sorry guys"

"Don't be stupid the important thing is, he knows we are ready for him now, he knows we will fight him back three on one" Gene said.

# CHAPTER 8:
## A PHONE CALL HOME

Cackling laughter echoed around the vast decadent indoor pool area of the Belle Vue Spa & Hotel, its tall curved arches decorated in luscious draping flower baskets framing the mural painted walls. All overseen by a stunning glass dome from above the pool which was almost the size of the whole room, around it on the sandy coloured stone flooring were bright white lounging chairs regimentally lined up. The Ladies had been celebrating for several hours now the announcement of Amy Jones's pregnancy

"Just look at her" Jenny said

"She will be saying goodbye to that stretch mark free stomach" she joked to Cara.

"Damn straight bless her, and good lord someone needs to tell those tits gravity exists" the two chuckled they weren't being mean or cruel they loved Amy she was sweet, kind and stunning both inside and out. *Blessed with a chest* – as Martha would say, she was a diddy little thing only about 5'7 with long brown hair – so long it came down to the top of her backside when she wore it down, but one thing was there for all to see she was glowing with complete contentment as she sat swishing her legs in the pool from the edge.

Martha whose scene this most certainly was not due to her *frumpiness* as she put it watched on as the others had been splashing around drunkenly in the pool apart from the gleaming mother to be of course, they had scared off the other guests as the night went on with their *raucous and uncouth behaviour* as the 'snooty bitch' as Cara called her had commented, this was referring to a woman who had been complaining to reception earlier in the night. Cara was one of those women that others looked at and thought *"I wouldn't mess with her",* she was very fitness orientated much like her husband Dennis, she also had short thick blonde hair which to many short sighted people meant she was either a metal head or a lesbian, but in reality she wasn't the roughian she looked to some just a little verbal.

As Amy sat by the edge of the pool Jenny wandered over and sat beside her nudging her shoulder to shoulder.

"Hey kiddo, you ok"

"Yeh just thinking about stuff, you know"

"It's natural to think about the bad happening again sweetie, but you have to look to the positives and you'll be fine so will little squirt" Jenny was like Amy in many ways just an older version of her and a tad taller, her twins who she had at a young age with a previous partner were off at college now so she was someone Amy knew she could ask for advice as there was no family here with them in the US.

"I wonder what them pesky boys are up to" Cara said.

"No good I'd imagine" Martha replied, to

which they all agreed

"I wonder if Hank managed to build that barbecue"

"Stu said the air was blue while he was trying and as usual he refused help" Jenny said

"He always does, I'm sure they rescued him in the end".

It was now 1am as the grand clock chimed in the large palatial lobby, most of the staff had retired for the evening bar Bob the old fella on reception he was working the graveyard shift and wasn't to bothered by the racket coming from the pool area down the hall as he could barely hear a word anyone said. He always sat with the radio news on, but he probably never heard a word being said apart from the odd tit-bit here and there.

"Ladies I am off to bed, I can't hack it like you can anymore" Martha said, a chorus of byes and goodnights rebounded around the room. She was the older of the women at 49 and her drinking days were well behind her which is how she liked it, walking down the hall way to the stairs which were in the lobby she looked at the pictures decorating the walls of various wealthy looking ladies and gentlemen from many generations ago.

"Goodnight" she said passing Bob who was fully enthralled in a book – The Slaughter House by a new author on the scene Jason McGovern, naturally he didn't hear her.

As Martha began to climb the steps something caught her ear, she turned abruptly and slipped a little down a step

"Excuse me can you turn that up ..." Bob looked up over the rim of his thick glasses perched on the tip of his nose.

"Oh hello dear can I help you"

"Can you turn the radio up please?"

"Ah – hard of hearing huh, you should get that checked out" he said turning up the volume.

"The tail end of hurricane Barry has caused vast damage and in some cases fatalities" the news reader continued listing names of areas affected by harsh weather storms, Martha's face dropped even more when she heard their small town could have been hit by the severe storms. She walked as fast as possible down the hallway bursting through the doors in to the pool room, the women screamed in shock before bursting into laugher.

"What's wrong?" Amy said noticing Martha looked terrified, the women soon snapped out of their fun loving mindsets and in to one of concern for what had worried Martha so much.

"There has been a really bad storm, and I think home may of been hit" she said, the others gasped and had that look of confused fear about them.

"We should call home, see if they are ok" Jenny said

"Yeh, yeh we have to" Cara agreed, they headed at haste down the hallway leaving wet footprints and on the exquisitely kept carpet runner.

"We need to use the phone please it's an emergency" Amy said as she stood at the reception desk, nothing Bob sat reading away.

"I think he is a little deaf" Martha said

"Hello I said can we use the phone please" Amy said raising her voice, Bob lifted his head slightly and his eyes widened as due to how he was sat his eyes were bang in line with Amy's chest and her white wet bikini looking right back at him

"S-Sorry dear what was that"

"The phone pal we have to use it now" Cara said reaching over and grabbing it, Bob gestured with his hands in a sort of sure go ahead motion. Jenny dialled her house

"Dead line" she said, Martha, Amy and Cara all tried with the same results.

"Oh god, what if –"

"Martha don't even think that way, there could be power issues because of the storm" Amy said as she hugged her sobbing fearful friend.

"The Police Station, call there see if they have phones up different grid area worth a shot" Cara said, in true Martha fashion she pulled a small book from her bag shuffled through the pages and handed it to Amy – sure enough in beautiful cursive writing it said *Sheriff Randy Skeets Office* and the number which Amy dialled.

"It's ringing" she said, the others hugged hopefully.

"Hello, you're through to –"

"Yes – hi I believe there is an issue at Vernon's Place and I –" Amy said at great speed.

"Ma'am, can I stop you there this is deputy Julie Dupont – now what's your name please"

"Amy – Amy Jones"

"Ok Amy , I need you to tell me slowly what's wrong"

"I am away from home, I tried calling but the phone lines are dead – I – I live on Vernon's Place"

"Vernon's with the Johnson's?"

"Yes, in fact I am with Martha right now she can't reach Hank either"

"Oh honey, if Hank is there he probably has them in a secret bunker" Deputy Dupont joked

"The power is probably down – a fallen tree or something, we will go check it out honey but could be a little while this storm has us spread thin"

"They could be hurt for god sake"

"Now I know you're scared but trust me if anything bad had happened someone would of gotten word to us now off the nearby streets or something, like I said we will check it out! Now where you stayin and I will call once I have an update"

"Don't bother" Amy said slamming the phone down and letting out a frustrated almost growl like sound

"The damn bitch wasn't arsed at all, they said they will check when they get chance"

"Let me guess Dupont?" Martha said

"Yep"

"She wouldn't rush if you walked in there with a knife in you and the person still holding on to it!"

"Right only one thing for it, we will drive home if Amy don't mind doing the driving that is as I have more wine in me than a vineyard" Cara said

"Sure I'll drive as long as everyone is cool with going back?" the others agreed.

"Bob ring up the bill please"

"Sure thing" he replied gazing into Amy's eyes like a schoolboy.

As the ladies packed their things, well more like crammed them into bags! they had the small TV's on in their rooms with some late night news on which had been extended to cover the storms sweeping through certain areas of the US.

"Death toll rises to 16" sent shudders down their spines as the reporter relentlessly updated every detail until silenced by the power off switch. The ladies regrouped in the lobby, Amy heading to the desk where Bob slid a white piece of paper with the hotel logo in golden print along the top, she never even looked at it just placed her credit card down

"Pay it on this please".

"Certainly Mrs Jones" Bob said.

"We will sort it out later" she said to the others.

"There we are then all done, I hope all is ok ladies and be carefully the roads will be a nightmare in these storms" Bob said as he smiled them off.

Outside they packed up Cara's 1974 Ford Ranch Wagon but not as neatly as before bags just crammed in even the precious shoe bag was forced into the boot with little care for its contents – so much so that one of the red shoes Cara had brought, the very same one Debbie Shultz had dreamed of owning fell out to the floor un-noticed by anyone and it sat in the now pouring rain as the group drove off.

# CHAPTER 9:
## AN UNKNOWN ENTITY

Water crashed and swilled around the kitchen sink of Stu Patterson's house, blood thinning as it disappeared down the plug hole while Gene tried to clean up Dennis's mangled nose which now resembled some sort of abstract art! bending and twisting in several directions a huge break in the middle and rather disgustingly a sharp piece of bone sticking out.

"ARRRGGHH, mother fucker – I am so glad I sliced that bastard's cheek open I tell you that"

"Nearly done son, nearly done" there was blood all over the cream tiled worktop with flower stencil patterns weaving around it framed in a stained oak edging it was a real country feeling kitchen.

"Ok while you're in here sorting him out I will go keep watch out front" Max said.

"And you're sure the wardrobe will block the broken window?"

"Yeh we will soon know if he moves that thing"

"Ok shout up if you need anything as will I" Gene said. As Max walked off to the lounge to keep watch as

Gene sat looking rather pensive, something clearly

troubling him.

"Right old man what's wrong" Dennis said

"Watch who you're calling old! It's nothing I am just over thinking things and creating thoughts that are impossible"

"Like what?"

Gene lowered his tone to just above a whisper

"Ok but you have to remember I don't believe this it's just something I thought about"

"Sure, totally, I get it"

"I was thinking about earlier when we thought Max may of" Gene paused

"Killed Stu, it got me thinking he is the only one not around when Hank, Alf and Stu died"

"None of us were together for Hank's death and we don't know when Alf died, but yeh he was the only one alive missing when Stu was killed" Dennis rested his forehead on his hand and sighed.

"It doesn't mean he's guilty but those three all died and he is the only one who was missing for the 3 even if we can't say for sure on the first two. And then there is the whole killer at his house for so long thing"

"You told me the torch was attached to a cat"

"That's what he told me, I never actually saw it myself" Gene said as he sat back a distressed look on his face.

"But he was with you the whole time so – unless, unless he is working with someone else and they are taking us out one by one"

"That's exactly where it led me, I mean in all honesty he's kind of an unknown entity to us. We know him from his time here but nothing previously apart from his sports career, for all we know he stood in that window and they had some sort of signal set up to tell the other guy someone was alone in a house"

"You're fucking right – I will fucking kill him" Dennis shot to his feet his chair falling to the ground with a scuffed clatter.

"Everything ok in there" Max shouted as low as possible from the lounge.

"Yeh no issues, Dennis got a little wobbly but he's ok now" Gene turned to Dennis

"Will you calm the hell down" he picked up the fallen chair and they sat back down.

"Calm down? That fucker has killed my friends"

"We don't know for sure, we have to find a way to be 100% positive before we act, after all there could be two men now not one"

The two men sat silently as they came to terms with the revelation that a man they trusted may be working against them, Dennis dabbing his nose gently with a wet rag to keep the blood at a minimum plainly becoming more and more agitated as the minutes passed by. Meanwhile in the lounge Max was sat watching the street unaware of the speculations brooding out back, he was however almost transfixed on the entrance to the sac and the faint but harrowing sight of his friend Stu's mangled broken corpse. His mind drifted to a couple of days previous when He and Amy visited Stu and Jenny's for dinner nothing over the top just some hotdogs while they watched the football but as Max recalled the evening he felt like he could never imagine feeling that happy again, realising how lucky they were that the wives had gone away but that itself caused a feeling of deep sorrow as they are blissfully unaware some of their lives are about to be shattered.

Looking around Stu's lounge at the pictures above the brick fireplace of their wedding day the sudden shudder of a branches shadow drew Max's attention to a splash of blood from Dennis's injuries on the floor, a thought exploded into his head he dashed to the kitchen startling the other men to their feet.

"You cut him right that's what you said"

"Yeh on cheek"

"Did you get him deep"

"I'm pretty sure it went right through, why?" Dennis said

"Blood! he would be pissing blood everywhere from the wound maybe just maybe there is some sort of trail" Gene and Dennis looked at each other with a look of suspicion in their eyes

"Think about it he is in a panic to get the hell out doesn't notice he's dropping it everywhere, but will be thinking about patching it up! Follow the trail catch the bastard"

"He's got a point" Gene said

"Damn right I do, come on out the back – quick" Max said heading for the door but the others didn't move

"What?"

"We aren't going anywhere until you answer a few things" Dennis said

"Guys come on we can get him"

"Listen to Dennis son, come on take a seat" Max frustratedly pulled out then slammed a chair down to sit on

"Ok what?"

"Now son don't take this to heart we just need clarify ..."

"Nah fuck that old timer, listen up Max there has been some shady shit going on tonight and I'm starting to think you have something to do with it" at that point Dennis revealed a large carving knife he had grabbed while sitting down.

"You fucking what mate? You're gunna pull a knife on me? You think I have been slaughtering my best mate and neighbours? You're fucking mental I have been with you two all night ..."

"But you haven't have ya! Sure all of us were supposedly alone when Hank died and fuck knows when he got Alf but out of us all you were the only one missing when Stu got his head sliced in half and then poof you fucking pop up again"

"You fucking ginger prick" Max flew to his feet his chair crashing across the room so fiercely it crashed into and broke through a cupboard door, Dennis rose up but Max grabbed a kitchen towel and almost like a magician swung it over the knife, grabbed Dennis's wrist and knocked him to the ground with a one hell of a left hook

"Never EVER point a knife at me again or I will fucking kill you"

"Put the knife down son" Gene said as Max grasped it tightly in his hand.

"Here take it" he handed it still in the towel to Gene

"I am not against you guys at all, you're my friends hell Stu was like family to me here" tears began to roll in droves down Max's face

"All I wanted was to be happy here with good people, my beautiful wife and kids some day. I want to find this fucker and end him I don't care if I have to go alone and you two stay here, I am going"

"Fine by me" Dennis said still on the floor

"I will go with him" Gene said much to the surprise of the other two

"Gene no stay here with Dennis, if I don't make it ..."

"Nah fuck that you going to grab your buddy to come take us out together no chance I go"

"Don't be stupid Dennis, you can barely stand without falling about all over the place I go with him end of"

"I tell you what I will go first into every room that way when he opens me up like a fish at least you will have a moment of realisation I was telling the truth before he gets you" Max said.

"Deal"

"Right let's get to it" Max said offering Dennis a hand to get up which he took.
The men prepared to head out the back taking knives and anything they could puncture a homicidal maniac with.

"I really should go alone, it don't feel right leaving Dennis here"

"I will be fine, besides anyone including you Maxwell comes in here without Gene and I will kill them,or you"

"Understood, be safe man"

"And you unless you're up to no good, in that case Gene here is under strict instructions to put a knife through the back of your skull"

"Well now the pep talk is over let's get this over with" Gene said picking up a hammer they had found in a kitchen draw.

The two men exited the back door, watched by Dennis they headed to around where the man would of climbed from the rear porch roof

"There" Gene said pointing to blood smeared on the guttering running around the porch, they scoured the mixture of grass and paving stones for blood it slowly led them past houses Dennis and then Max's houses.

"I'm pretty sure he's gone to mine" Gene said coming to a stop

"He would of seen the medical kit in the kitchen for sure when he – when he killed Alf"

"Ok we will check past Hanks to be safe first" Max said as he began leading the way, they reached number 4 there was no blood leading to the house but through the window they could make out Hank's gut still suspended from the ceiling.

By now the splashes and drops of blood were getting lesser and harder to see on grass and in darkness, but they did lead seemingly to Gene's house. They approached slowly across the damp grass it made a faint crunch noise underfoot, Max stopped at the side of the door and gently pressed on it and it moved slightly signalling it was open. Gene put his finger to his lips to signal keep quiet to which Max nodded and then gestured he was going in, the door opened slowly into the silent almost peaceful kitchen as Max gently stepped in followed cautiously by Gene. As they almost glided through the kitchen due to treading so lightly, they entered the large lobby Max signalled to stop they stood as he looked around a carving knives poised for action. It helped that all the houses in the cul-de-sac were identical in layout so when you have staggered around one in the pitch black at night getting in from a bar you've basically staggered around them all, he gestured with a slight head movement that he was moving on. He passed the dining room glancing into it as he did, then a clattering noise came from behind he swung around and Gene was gone and the basement door under the stairs was open

"Gene" he whispered, a very nervous and deep breath followed and with knife poised he slowly approached the doorway.

"Hey" a voice whispered from behind, Max turned swinging the knife but no one was there, he turned back towards the doorway just as a hooded head smashed into his knocking him out cold.

# CHAPTER 10:
# LET ME FIX YOU

Slumped in the corner of Stu and Jenny's lounge throwing back some whisky and painkillers he'd found in the kitchen like he was popping candy and drinking lemonade Dennis watched both entrances intently while woozily swaying around in his chair.

"If I am going out you cowardly fuck I am doing it in style" he said raising a glass and spilling most of the contents over himself and the floor.

"Oopsy, Jenny won't be best pleased about that" he looked at a picture of Stu in his pressed grey wedding suit atop the mantel piece as he said it.

"Here's to you old friend" taking a sip

"Empty for god sake" he snatched the bottle from the floor and filled his glass again loosing count of how many he'd had.

"Th- Th- These people don't understand the bond Stu, ya know. You was my friend a long time before Mr Soccer Star and The Tits moved in, s-s-sure you became close to them but me and you buddy – pals t-t-to the end" the glass dropped to the floor and rolled in an almost perfect circle until it hit the chair leg and came to a stop, the tremble of a very drunken man with a severely broken nose snoring began to fill the room – Dennis had passed out.

With a deep breath and a jolt Dennis sat bolt upright in the chair almost slipping off the edge, he looked in the direction of the stairs just past the lounge sure that he had heard the creek of the floorboards upstairs. He sat silently slowly reaching down for the large butchers knife he had acquired while 'Tooling Up' as Max called it, just as he began to think he imagined it the noise came again.

"Time for round two fucktard" he whispered lifting himself to his feet with a sway and a slight stagger, he approached the stairs and cautiously looked round to check the coast was clear before gently creeping up the stairs. With every creek and clank they made he would stop moving and brace in case the man attacked, as he reached the top he looked down the hall way at the end of which stood the wardrobe covering the broken window – it's door clattered from the inside slightly.

"Fuck, fuck, fuck" Dennis whispered as he took a large gulp and deep breath, he grasped the knife so hard his wrist cracked – *meow* – came from the wardrobe and a scratching noise.

"Jesus fucking Christ you little shit, I am preparing for war and this stupid cat is in the damn cupboard" he marched to the wardrobe and slung the doors open – the cat launched into his face, clawing at him even catching the bone from his nose.

He staggered back trying to rip the cat from his face as he grabbed at the animal he felt attached to it was a small head torch and realised Max had been telling the truth. As he got to the top of the stairs he managed to toss the cat down them, he stood almost breathless looking down as the cat screeched and ran off, he turned to go and retrieve the knife he dropped in the panic but as he did the man in black pushed him down the stairs, his head thudded off the steps and banister as he crashed helplessly down them his arm slipped through the banister and the snap of it breaking echoed in the open space as he screamed before smashing his head on the hard floor rendering him unconscious.

"Deary me Dennis you are in a state, best let me fix you" the man said as he lifted him from under the shoulders and began dragging him to the kitchen.

*What's that smell?* – Dennis thought as he began to come around, then in a flash the memory of what happened sparked to life and he went to move but was met with unbearable pain from his right arm, he looked at it with his weary eyes and saw his Humerus bone sticking out of his arm with skin and parts of his shirt hanging from it like a limp flag on its pole in a heat wave.

A ruff muffled voice came from besides him

"I know, not very humorous is it" and laugher boomed around the room.

"Fuck you" Dennis growled through blood, tears and snot

"Fuck you, you coward"

"That's just not very nice Dennis, but respect has never been your strong point has it? Let's face it that is probably why your pal Stu – god rest his soul, went off with the newbie's because well you're an ass hole" the man bent down to come face to face with Dennis who spat flem and blood towards his eyes and tried to headbutt him but failed as he was tied tightly to a kitchen chair.

"Now, now Dennis, believe it or not I want to help you out little. You have really been through the wars my man so I feel I have a duty to help, so I say to you sir let me fix you"

"Go fuck yourself"

"Maybe later when all this is done" the man said.

Dennis watched as the man rummaged in a small zip bag he had.

"It's amazing what that fat shit Hank had knocking around, some really helpful stuff" he said pulling out a small hand saw

"Like this little beauty, just what we need"

"Wh-what the fuck you on about"

"I told you, I am going to fix you. Now I need something for the pain – ah, here we go" he pulled out a manky old cloth and rammed it in Dennis's mouth

"I can't work with screams they are so brain melting. Funny story Debbie Shultz had that rammed in her mouth just before I killed her and faked her little car boo boo"

Dennis's face turned to one of sheer terror, he started trying to slam his feet up and down and wriggle about desperate for a bit of luck to break free, but his arm hurt too much so he began sobbing, as drool and snot streamed from his face.

"I always wanted to make that bitch gag but not like that, you know what I'm saying" the man laughed

"Now I hate to tell you this Dennis but that nose is well – fucked my friend and you aint going to look pretty with it once it heals, if it ever does. So I have a plan just sit back and relax let Doctor Dark here work his magic" as Dennis squirmed and tried to scream for help which was just muffled groans due to the gag, the man grabbed the back of his hair to hold his head in place – raised the handsaw to the top of Dennis's nose and began to move it back and forth pressing down. Blood sprayed aimlessly in the air the squelching, ripping and tearing of flesh and tissue sounded like that annoying person who eats in a quiet room and swills the food around their mouth with saliva. Dennis's yelling from behind the gag his body stiff as a gravestone in shock, bone snapping crunching and squeaking as the saw shuddered through it.

Dennis was now in a state of near unconsciousness, if not for the booze and painkillers earlier he surely would have passed out a long time ago. He could hear some muffled sounds which were likely the man talking at him but he couldn't make anything out.

"Hey, hey come on Dennis keep with me man nearly all sorted fella" the man said as he removed the gag.

"P-P-Please S-Stop"

"I'm helping you don't be ungrateful" the man placed a large silver container on the table in front of Dennis who could just about make out a blurry shiny object.

"I have been thinking fella, I can't leave that nose open like that we need something hot to seal the wound ya know" Dennis coughed and blood squirted from the nose hole

"See that shit proves it, luckily good ol'reliable Stu has one of these fat fryer gizmo's"
Dennis shook his head

"No please don't"

"Relax its up to the boil, one more moment of pain and then bingo wound sealed all happy again" the man began whistling away as he began cleaning off the handsaw.

"Why are you doing this to us all" Dennis said

"Why? Why Dennis? Why not I say, you see you all think you are the cocks of the walk, strutting about spending your money trying to outdo each other. Yet here I come and just like that I wipe you all out one by one, was it all worth it?"

"If you had come at us like a man, we would of fucked you up any of us would and then you sad little prick I'd of personally paid a couple of guys to butt fuck you to hell" Dennis again spat towards the man.

"Well, maybe you would have – we will never know now will we" the man stood up and grasped the back of the chair

"Hot damn I nearly forgot, I best show you who has saved your face, just in case – you know, you don't make it" the man leant to the side of Dennis who turned to look him in the eyes, the man slowly pulled the cover from the lower part of his face – Dennis stared in shock for a moment

"You?" he said "You were fuc –" at that point the man grabbed Dennis's hair tilted the chair and plunged his face into the deep fat fryer, popping and sizzling accompanied by the screams faintly coming from under the fat was like music to the man's ears. Dennis was convulsing and wriggling for quite a bit of time until he stopped and went limp.

"Shit left him too long – oh well" the man let the body go and it fell to the floor dragging the fryer with it hot fat crashing everywhere as the man walked away leaving the burned blistered and broken corpse of Dennis behind.

The man stepped out into the silent cul-de-sac just the drips from branches and roofs pattering in the background and a slight rustling from the winds. The skies had slightly started to lighten as 5am was approaching and the sun would be lighting up the massacre site around 6, he headed to Hanks which had his large truck on the driveway, he drove it over to the trees blocking the road. Taking the thick tow cable he attached it to one them and tightened the slack, then removing Hanks keys from his pocket which he had taken earlier he put the truck in reverse, it clunked and chugged a little the tyres slipping on the slick surface but he managed to shift the tree enough to get a car through.

"Right lets finish this, after all its rude to keep guests waiting" he said as he strolled casually over to Gene's where the last of the residents awaited him unconsciously on the basement floor.

# CHAPTER 11:
## AS THE DUST SETTLES

Max's mouth and lips felt dry as he coughed and dust exploded into the air as he lay aching on a cold lumpy concrete floor, his eyes squinted open as the dust slowly cascaded back down irritating his eyes as it did. His vision began to seep through the groggy haze as his body ached from lying on the cold hard floor for god knows how long. As Max's focus returned he could tell he was in the basement of Gene's home, he tried to move his arms and legs but they had been tied up so he struggled and managed to wriggle onto his side as each heavy breath caused a small dust storm.

"Gene" he whispered

"Gene are you here, are you ok?"

Nothing but deadly silence flooded the room, as he looked around the dark dank brick basement he noticed Alf's beat up old hunting repairs desk in the corner and on it some old blades which may of been blunt but right now that was the best thing since sliced bread in Max's dust filled eyes, he began to cautiously roll over. If he could get over and use the wall to help shuffle to his knees, he could then grab a blade in his teeth and drop it behind him to pick up and cut free.

As he reached the bench he over egged the final roll and hit the desk which screeched as it scuffed on the concrete, Max froze for a few moments but nothing happened the coast was clear. He began to shuffle into a sitting position scrapping the skin from his hands on the floor as he did, then he hotched over to the wall pressed his back hard against it and pushed his feet solidly to the floor and with every ounce of strength pushed, he groaned as he began to rise from the floor his back sliding up the jagged brick wall and shuffling his feet closer to it as he did – then to his amazement he realised he had managed to stand up, he let out a small joyous laugh and hopped a few steps over to the desk he leant in to pick a blade up in his teeth and noticed a white sheet of paper, on it was written *Well done Max, I didn't give you due credit! I never thought you'd get this far!* Max's stomach sank and he was suddenly yanked back and thrown to the floor.

"Shit me that was fucking intense!"
Max looked up through the cloud of dust to see the man in black stood in front of him.

"I stood in this dark little corner right behind you, my asshole was twitching in case you saw me the whole time! I mean what's that all about? You're tied up not me and I was shitting it!" The man laughed as he grabbed an old beer crate and placed it down to sit on.

"What have you done with Gene"

"Oh don't you worry, you will see soon enough kiddo"

"Why are y –"

"Why are you doing this, why us, why here, for god sake don't you people every get new material! Fuuuck Mee! It's so dull when you want to know the same old shit all the damn time" the man had a gratingly condescending tone to his voice, as he gestured dramatically like a sulky teenager being told they can't go to the local party.

"Fine, I will mix it up for you – why the fuck are you so cowardly you hide your face and run around in the shadows? Afraid I could fuck you up?"

"Woo-hoo-hoo, sheesh the attitude in that was inspiring kiddo" the man slapped his knee in what seemed like excitement.

"You see that's the shit right there, and for that I'm going to reward you" The man stood up and removed his gloves.

"The others they only got this little gem just as they left the world but as this is now the endgame, well you get to see now!"

The man removed his hood and then the mask covering the bottom of his face, Max's jaw dropped in pure shock.

"ALF!" he yelled.

"Ha ha, no one ever suspects the dead guy Max!"

"But Gene saw you, he saw you dead"

"You ever played dead kiddo? It's a fucking breeze in a panic pot like this"

"What have you done to Gene?" Max snarled through gritted teeth, spit shooting from his mouth as he did.

"Awww are you worried about American Daddy? Well I told you all in good time, you'll love it!"

Alf went over to a filthy cracked mirror on the wall and inspected the huge gash he had stitched up on his face.

"Dennis?" Max asked.

"He's had a hard day, he's totally fried that fella"

"What did you do?" Max sounded defeated, completely heartbroken knowing he was probably the last resident there alive.

"I cut his fucking nose off and boiled his head in a fryer, Unlucky really as it was down to you two as to who won the main prize"

"What fucking prize you deranged old bastard"

"DO NOT call me old, I will fucking end you right here you little shit" Alf screamed and punched the mirror smashing what was left of it to pieces.

"You know what Max, I am fucked if I can be arsed to piss about anymore I'm sorry but the games done!" Alf pulled a large hunting knife from the back of his trousers and lunged towards Max, but was pushed to the side – by Gene.

"Gene, fuck this prick up" Max said with elation beaming from his voice.

"What the hell are you doing Alf?"

"He called me old again Gene, HE CALLED ME OLD!"

"Gene, kill him for fuck sake he's a mental old fucker who should of been locked up!"

"Now that is no way to speak of your elder's son" Gene said as he reached a hand out to help Alf up to his feet.

"Gene? What ..."

"For a while I thought Dennis was going to kill you and he would be the final player left, I mean I pushed all his buttons but you were fucking amazing at slapping him down! That shit with the towel and the knife was ninja level amazing"

"You – you were in it together? Of course you were, you told me Alf was dead, you stopped me checking and you led me here leaving Dennis alone" Max shook his head trying to fathom out how he didn't realise.

"Son I even dropped hints but you two never even noticed! I told you about the two killers I said how they told the young cop it was a game to them how would I know that if he was killed, unless –"

"Unless you were the killers, my god you literally fucking told me"

"Don't beat yourself up kiddo you aint the first to miss it" Alf said as he was changing into some more regular clothes.

"You did finish Dennis right Gene?"

"Oh yeh he smelt like fried chicken when I was done" Gene grinned proudly as he looked towards Max and winked.

"But Alf said ..."

"Well I couldn't ruin the surprise could I Max, so I told you I did it" Alf shrugged his shoulders as if this was a perfectly obvious and normal reason.

"Who the fuck are you two?"

The men stopped and exchanged looks, and then un-nerving smiles. Gene went over to the work bench and opened the small cabinet underneath, from it he retrieved and old biscuit tin the colour and pattern had all but rusted off. He prised it open and removed some tatty newspaper clippings and held them one by one for Max to see the headlines, each one was a small town name followed by words like massacre, slaughter and bloodfest. Gene placed the clippings back in the tin and sat it on the floor in the corner, Alf then lit a match and tossed it in the tin.

"Shame to do this but needs must " he said and the tin glowed with flames dancing from it.

"That still doesn't explain who the fuck you are" Max said. The two men sat Max up against the wall and pulled the beer crate and an old cooler box over to perch on.

"Ok son, as you made it this far we will let you in on a little secret" Gene said placing a hand on Max's leg, which he wriggled to try and get away from.

"Yeh fuck it, I mean not like it's going to matter" Alf said.

"You know you lot always said we look alike, well that's because we are brothers" Gene said as Max looked on in disbelief.

"You see Alf here was always a little different as a kid, our father tried to beat it outta him and failed. One day he beat him for an hour straight, Alf just laughed and laughed it enraged the drunken bastard. Mom came home and tried to get him to stop but he turned on her instead and smashed her head in with the fridge door"

"My god"

"I know Max, what a prick! So Alf saw his chance and smashed a chair over the old man's head, but couldn't leave it there so he gauged his eyes out with a spoon and stamped on his bollocks until they were crushed. After that we ran, we were about 16 at the time but we were street smart" Gene said patting Alf on the back.

"After that we got a taste for it, we drifted from place to place seeing what we could get away with"

"Hey Gene, remember that black fucker near Kentucky trying to make it with that pretty white girl the waitress" Alf said as he sniggered.

"How could I not she had the biggest pair of titties I'd ever seen, until you cut them off and wore them as a hat!"

"Yeh that fucker got a public hanging for her murder" Alf laughed as Max looked on in disgusted shock.

"H-How did you end up here?"

"Well that fucking cop I told you about, that was a wakeup call that we'd gotten sloppy and maybe it was time to start a fresh, I mean it was getting a bit old and we didn't get the trills as much"

"So we settled down" Alf said winking at Max, he then got up and started rummaging through some rope testing it for length and strength.

"We came across these two soldiers, pretty similar to us we got chatting to them in a bar, they told us about their lives and their mothers back home that were pretty old and bit stupid you know how it is. Anyway we arranged to go fishing with them the next day as we hit it off, we met them by the lake had some laughs drank a few beers, slit their throats and chopped them up for fish bait!"

"They must of tasted fucking great we caught more fish than a trawler!" Alf shouted from the back of the room where he was amassing a mountain of rope.

"Once they were gone we slipped on their uniforms and became Gene and Alf from Vernon's Place"

"Didn't people know you weren't them?" Max asked.

"Nah, their mothers were old poor sighted and hadn't seen them for so long they couldn't remember what they looked like anyway. And everyone else had moved on by this point, so we kept them around for a bit then took a pillow to them one at a time and that was that no more questions could ever be raised about Gene and Alf"

Max could barely process what he was hearing, he replayed things over in his mind as Gene watched the dying embers of the clippings fade away in the now scorched tin.

"What about your wives? You must of been settled?"

"Oh we were, we had landed the best lives. Gene and Alf – the real ones that is, had big old payouts and pensions to collect! A few forged documents and we were laughing" Gene then pulled his wallet out and from it a picture of the two of them along with Gladys and Mary he held it so Max could see.

"They were great – until about 10 years ago when we had to get rid of them"

"What a god damn circus show that shit was" Alf said as he returned to sit on the cooler with a large thick rope in hand.

"W-W-Why did you h-have to kill them?" Max asked

"Well about 6 years before that Alf got the urge to have some fun again shall we say, and to cut a long story short we murdered a couple of fishermen camping out by the lake"

"That shit was fun we toyed with them for hours" Alf said

"Unfortunately, that nosey little bitch that lived in your house eventually somehow found out, so we slaughtered her family and then made it look like she killed them and herself"

"That was so good being right there in the thick
of it police all over the street, and us pair guilty as sin fooling them all!" Alf jumped up clapped his hands and headed up stairs.

"So the years went on and Alf started to get itchy again and one night when he was drunk and bragged to Gladys about it, she tried to run but he stopped her kept her in doors and slowly poisoned her until she died of what seemed like natural causes"

"Jesus, Gene he's a psycho! At least you seem to at least have some grasp on reality"

"Maybe but it didn't stop me doing the same to Mary, she had to go I needed to keep Alf close to stop him getting out of hand. So she died and he moved in, that was that" Gene placed the photo back in his wallet and returned it to his pocket.

"So who are you really?" Max said

"It's been so long I barely remember, but my name was Bobby Helms and Alf was Ted"

"Bobby and Teddy huh, sound like a pair of pussies, you never were in the army were you?" Max said glaring at Gene.

"Were we balls! Some stuck up buzz cut pricks bossing us about? No chance!"

"So why do this now after so long? Why not stay retired live out your lives?"

"Well son ..."

"Don't call me son"

"Sorry – son. Those other fuckers were getting on our tits, treating us like useless old men so we decided one last hurrah so to speak show them what old men could do. But we needed a fall guy and unknown entity in the mix and when that prick tease Debbie told me about you we were ready to go"

"You killed her didn't you?"

"Oh yeh I fucking sliced her throat in half"

"You fucking bastard she was innocent!"

"DON'T YOU DARE TELL ME THAT! She was a prick teasing hoar!" Gene shot up and kicked the cooler across the basement.

"Gene you ok down there?" Alf shouted from above.

"Yeh just Max pissing me off"

Gene paced back and forth for a few moments muttering under his breath before taking a large gulp of air and forcing a grin to his face.

"The worst part is Max, I like you I really do! That's why I was trying to get Dennis to kill you but I guess it wasn't meant to be. You never treated us like old men and for that thank you son"

"Fuck you old man"

Gene punched Max hard across the face.

"Don't push it son! Ginger sack didn't pull through so you are who takes the fall"

"The fall?"

"Oh yeh kiddo you are the Vernon's Place Killer!" Alf said as he returned through the door.

"We are again going to be hidden in plain sight! A few minor wounds but us two old fucks killed the killer"

"Over my dead body" Max snarled

"Yeh – that's the point! Gene we are ready upstairs we best get this done suns coming up fast"

"Sorry Son" Gene said as he whacked Max's head against the wall knocking him out cold.

# CHAPTER 12:
# AN AMERICAN DREAM, FULL OF NIGHTMARES

"Wake him up" Gene said as Alf held Max using rope tightly pulled around his throat, he shook him from side to side.

"Wakey, Wakey"

Max began to come around, soon realising he was like a dog on a leash. He noticed he was now in the garage surrounded by gardening tools and fishing equipment, his back and head hurt like hell.

"Argh, my back" he said followed by the realisation he was no longer tied up apart from the tight grasp of Alf holding rope around neck.

"Don't try anything kiddo or I will pull back and kick down so fast your spine will shatter in half" Alf said pressing his head to Max's.

"Now get up nice and steady"

"Why – Argh – Why does my back hurt so fucking much?"

"We were a tad concerned you would try something on the stairs so we knocked you out and dragged you up them with the rope – sorry about that son" Gene said standing in front of the other two with a large hunting knife in his hand.

As Alf who was still holding firmly on Max's leash talked to Gene about what was to happen next Max zoned out staring at a random draw in the garage his mind drifted to the dream he had where the child told him he left them, was he referring to what was to come – Max's death? A tear rolled down his cheek.

"Max you still with us son"

"I don't have much choice do I!"

"Huh, not really" Gene laughed

"For the record, we won't hurt the women, on that you have my word"

"Your word? Your fucking word? You can take that and cram it up your ass you old fuck"
Alf tightened the rope around Max's neck his eyes bulged and flem spewed from his gritted teeth.

"ENOUGH!" Gene shouted as Alf loosened his grip a little.

"I can let it slide given what's coming next, I am sorry son but we have to do you in, and then sort our heroic injuries out. Alf you got him good?"

"Oh yeh, stick the fucker!"
Gene held the knife up in line with Max's chest, who stood staunchly a look of defiance on his face.

"I am sorry son" Gene said coming forwards the knife held firmly towards Max.

"You will be" Max snarled as he pushed both feet off the floor and into Gene's stomach kicking him backwards over a table in the garage, and in turn thrusting himself and Alf backwards with a stiff thud. Max fell to the floor his shoulder in agony he looked towards it and it was bleeding heavily from a large cut just to the side of his neck, he noticed the rope was on the floor Alf had let go! He looked up to see him stood against a support pillar in the garage with a blood covered rusted blade of a set of garden edging shears through his left eye his body twitching slightly.

"Alf? You killed him" Gene said his voice trembling with emotion, Max rose to his feet and turned his head to Gene who was now without his blade. He glared at him for a moment a flicker of fear flashed on Gene's face as he gulped in a large breath.

"It's over Max, he's gone I don't have to –"

"Don't have to what? Kill me? Lie to every single wife who's husband you murdered? Deprive an unborn child of its father? Tell me Ge – Bobby what don't you have to do?"

"I – I don't have to listen to your whiny ass" Gene threw a fishing tackle box which knocked Max back and over a tool box on the floor, Gene then ran from the garage. Max clambered to his feet and ran out after him, he came out past the car a leg flew out from in front of it sending Max face first into the coarse stony road surface. Gene then smashed his foot down on Max's back driving his ribs down a cracking noise followed by an agonising scream followed, and then he kicked Max in the side of his ribs he rolled down to the gutter where he lay groaning and coughing which caused more agony.

"You thought you could stop me? I have been doing this for 50 years you little prick! I've murdered more men than you've seen titties boy" Gene gave another kick to the ribs.

"May-Maybe y-y-you have, but I killed your bitch brother" Max said almost breathlessly as he wheezed his words out.

"That is unfortunate, but then it just leaves the sole survivor which may be more believable that us both making it again! Plus now I don't have to watch over him all the time, so in a way you've probably done me a favour!"

"A-And I thought you w-were the saner one"

Gene laughed as he breathed in the fresh morning breeze, the sun breaking its way through the clouds and trees, he spotted a metal meat skewer on the floor that must of been missed during the barbecue clear up which he picked up.

"Right, get up son"

"Fuck you"

"Well if you wanna die in the gutter that's fine with me, but I was at least going to let you stand like a man and take it" Gene moved towards Max who was looking over his shoulder.

"Fine, wait – I will get up" Max managed to struggle to his knees but stopped and began breathing heavily, Gene stood behind him.

"Come on son, up you pop or I will do it right now. I need my number one fall guy"

"Like I said, OVER MY DEAD BODY" Max sprung to his feet and swung round smashing the crowbar that had been knocked out of his hands earlier that night by Dennis across Gene's face, teeth sprayed across the road and the skewer clattered away from him as he crashed to the floor. He went to crawl towards the skewer but Max slammed the crowbar down shattering his ankle, Gene screamed in agony and rolled onto his back.

"P-Please s-s-son stop I will confess the lot just stop" he said and lay helplessly on the floor raising his hand up to try and calm Max down.

"What were the insurances Alf spoke of?"

"Th-that was bull shit, to keep you all here"

"You mean we stayed, people died based on

more LIES!" Max said through gritted teeth.

Max began breathing erratically his body shaking with rage, he gripped the crowbar so tightly his fingers cracked as they tightened and with a roar akin to a bears he plunged it down into Gene's skull his head caved instantly as his eyes bulged out from their sockets – the force caused his remaining teeth to crunch down severing his tongue and shattering them at the same time. Max drew back and again thudded down on his skull, the right side shattered as brain oozed out onto the road then again and again Max slammed the crowbar down crunching and pulverising Gene's skull.

"FREEZE!" a woman's voice echoed around the cul-de-sac, followed by the clicking of a gun being readied to fire.

"Freeze right now or I will shot!" Max stopped, his breathing more erratic than ever, blood dripping from his face which had sprayed on him, the black crowbar now crimson with blood dribbled into the gutter. He focussed on the woman, it was Dupont, she had kept to her word when she told Amy she would check in on them as soon as they had availability, unfortunately it was too late.

"Sir drop the weapon and lie face down on the ground" Dupont said as other squad cars arrived and officers cautiously stepped passed the fallen trees guns fixed on Max.

"Max?" the soft voice of Amy crept from behind the officers. She stepped out into his sight, he dropped to his knees shaking his head.

"I – I didn't ..." he whispered as a scream chilled the spines of everyone nearby.

"STUART!" Jenny yelled as she tried to run over to his blood soaked body, but officers grabbed her.

"We have another one here" an officer shouted from the direction of Stu's house referring to Dennis, Cara dropped to her knees like she could sense it was him. Then as Martha stood tears filling her eyes she saw an officer run from her house and throw up on the porch, she closed her eyes forcing the tears down her cheeks.

Dupont and Officer Graves approached Max and cuffed him, Dupont began reading him his rights but all he heard was mumblings he was just fixated on the lonely heartbroken figure of Amy stood rigid as tears rolled down her beautiful soft skin her heart shattering as she watched the man she loved being chained up.

"- do you understand sir?" Dupont asked.

"Sir?"

"I didn't do anything" Max said softly.

"Well everyone is dead but you sir, so that tells me otherwise" Dupont and Graves picked him up and placed him not so gently into the back of a squad car.

"Johnson, call for medical he will need attention and probably a hospital visit" Dupont said.

"Medical? Fucking medical? Bitch are you on drugs that fucker murdered everyone here! Let me finish his ass off!" Cara said being held back by two female officers.

"Cara I ..." Amy said.

"Amy shut the hell up, your husband is a psychopath, and right now I'm wondering if you're in on this! I mean after all you talked us in to leaving here!"

"Cara!" Martha snapped.

"Look at the poor woman she has lost her husband like we have" Martha fell to her knees crying as Amy and then Cara comforted her.

"Amy I'm so ..."

"No, don't say it you have every right to feel that way" The three hugged on the damp pathway as Jenny was being consoled by trainee Olivia Sandwell, who god bless her was on day three of her Police training.

By now crowds had began to amass at the entrance to Vernon's Place due to the loud sirens and flashing lights, the ambulance struggled to gain entry along with the forensics vans.

"Get him to that ambulance, if he tries anything Graves smash the prick in the ribs, Johnson you go with him" Dupont said as she eyed Max in the back of the squad car. Amy watched as he was man handled from the car to the ambulance, he looked broken, distant and a shadow of the man she had left a few days before. The ambulance left for the hospital with Graves and Johnson in the back alongside Max who was cuffed to the bed, Officer Tully followed in a squad car for back up.

As the hours passed by Max who was now cuffed to a rather uncomfortable hospital bed under heavy guard watched the clock ticking by minute by minute, and at exactly 7:03pm the door crept open and in walked Amy.

"You have ten minutes ma'am" Officer Johnson said as he closed the door.

"Hi" she said softly as she walked over to the bed.

"Amy I di ..."

"Stop it Max, no more lies. They found the ID of a woman from Minnesota that went missing about six months ago while she was travelling and I was away at the beach with Jenny for a few days in a tin under the bedroom floorboards! The poor woman's body was found butchered about 30 miles away from here – HOW COULD YOU!" she yelled.

"Amy I swear to you I didn't do it, they must of planted them"

"They? They who Max?"

"Gene and Alf they weren't even ..."

"NO! ENOUGH!"

"You have to believe me Amy I would never lie to you I swear"

"Swear on our unborn babies life then, if you are so truthful then do that" Amy said turning away tears streaming from her eyes.

"I – I swear, on our unborn babies life I never committed those murders or killed our friends" Max sobbed as tears soaked his pillow.

Amy straightened up her back still facing Max, she wiped the tears from her face before turning to look at him.

"You are a vile, inhuman monster! You would lie on your own child's life? You deserve to fry for this Max! I was so happy here but now it's just an American dream, full of nightmares! God knows if those poor women will ever speak to me again after this I HATE YOU – I HATE YOU!!"

"Please, Amy I wouldn't, I'm your husband"

Max tried to sit up but the cuffs tightened and pulled him back down.

"No, no you are not my husband, I have no idea what you are! But you are definitely not the man I married! Goodbye" Amy turned to walk away opening the door and stepping through it.

"Amy, please ..."

"Goodbye" she whispered as the door closed.

# ABOUT THE AUTHOR

At 36 this is my first ever attempt at writing, truth be told I have never been a reader and until recently I hadn't willingly finished a book! I say willingly as we were forced to at school. I lacked the patience and attention span to do it until I went down a rabbit hole watching YouTube videos probably starting with something like 'Funny Dog Videos' and somehow ending up several hours later clicking on a Stephen King talk. I was curious as obviously I had heard of him, but had never really seen much of him and IT had been re made and was set for release so I watched on and instantly was inspired! I signed up to Audible and amassed a large library of books from Mr. King and Brandon Sanderson.

For years I had ideas swilling around in my head of stories I would tell myself when I couldn't sleep or when I got bored at work – that happened a lot. So after watching several hours of Stephen King talks and interviews I sat in front of my computer with one idea a cul-de-sac in the USA where someone starts killing people that was it, that was all I had. But as I typed it turned into what you have just read, the best moment was when my wife sat and read the first ten chapters and we sat on the bed talking about the whole thing she had been hooked and totally surprised by how much she enjoyed it and couldn't wait to see the final chapters unfold.

It may be a cliché and corny but I was honestly inspired by Stephen King's talks and his approach that he is just a normal guy who writes stories that people like and he gets a kick out of terrifying them too. Thank you to those who read this book and to those who do and hate it – at least I did it.

Printed in Great Britain
by Amazon